Lucy's Butterfly Garden

Freya Jobe

Published by Freya Jobe, 2024.

This is a work of fiction. Similarities to real people, places, or events are entirely coincidental.

LUCY'S BUTTERFLY GARDEN

First edition. October 27, 2024.

Copyright © 2024 Freya Jobe.

ISBN: 979-8227677129

Written by Freya Jobe.

Lucy's Butterfly Garden

Lucy loved all things bright and beautiful, but nothing fascinated her more than butterflies. She could spend hours watching them flutter by, marveling at their colorful wings and the way they danced through the air. But Lucy didn't just want to watch butterflies; she dreamed of creating a special place where they would come to visit her every day. She wanted a garden filled with flowers of every color, where butterflies would feel safe, welcome, and at home.

One warm summer afternoon, after a magical dream about a garden bursting with butterflies, Lucy shared her big idea with her family. With a spark of excitement and a sprinkle of determination, Lucy decided to turn her dream into reality. She was going to create her very own butterfly garden, a place where caterpillars could grow and butterflies could soar.

But Lucy had no idea where to start. She'd never grown a garden before, and she didn't know the first thing about taking care of butterflies. Yet, with a heart full of wonder and a mind buzzing with questions, Lucy set out on an adventure of learning and discovery. Along the way, she'd make friends, face challenges, and discover that with a little patience and a lot of love, anything is possible—even growing a magical garden for butterflies.

Lucy's Butterfly Garden is a story about dreams, discovery, and the magic of nature. Join Lucy as she builds her garden, one flower and one butterfly at a time, and learns that sometimes, the best gardens grow not just from seeds, but from the heart.

Chapter 1: The Magical Dream

The sun was setting outside as Lucy lay in bed, snuggled up under her favourite soft blanket. She closed her eyes, letting her thoughts drift away, her mind swimming with the sights and sounds of a perfect summer day. She could still feel the warmth of the sun on her face, the tickle of grass under her feet, and the gentle breeze that had carried the scent of flowers. Soon, her breathing grew steady, and Lucy drifted into a deep, peaceful sleep.

As she slept, a strange yet beautiful world unfolded around her, one that seemed almost real. Lucy found herself standing in a garden, but not just any garden—a garden like nothing she had ever seen before. Flowers taller than she was stretched out in every direction, their colors so vibrant they looked as if they were painted by the sun itself. Pinks, purples, yellows, and blues—each bloom looked more magical than the last, and the air was alive with the scent of fresh blossoms.

Lucy's eyes sparkled as she took it all in. She stepped forward, her feet sinking into the soft, mossy ground. Then, as if by some invisible cue, the garden came alive. Butterflies—dozens, no, hundreds of them—began to flutter around her, their delicate wings brushing against her skin as they danced through the air. Each one was unique, with colors and patterns Lucy had never imagined. Some were deep blues with shimmering silver spots, others were bright yellow with specks of orange, and a few even had hints of pink, like petals of a sunset.

Lucy held out her hands, watching in awe as a small, delicate butterfly, with wings the color of a summer sky, landed gently on her finger. She could feel its tiny legs against her skin, and she marvelled at how soft and light it felt, as if it were barely there. She wanted to say something, to thank the butterfly for choosing her, but words seemed unnecessary. She simply stood still, her heart filled with joy.

The garden around her was so peaceful, and Lucy felt completely at home. It was as if she belonged in this magical place, surrounded by these creatures who trusted her without hesitation. A soft hum filled the air, a gentle song that seemed to come from the garden itself, and Lucy felt a deep sense of happiness and wonder.

As she walked slowly through the garden, butterflies drifted beside her, some darting ahead to lead the way while others seemed content to linger by her side. She noticed plants she'd never seen before, with leaves as big as her head and flowers that seemed to glow softly in the dimming light. There were tiny puddles nestled between the flowers, where butterflies would occasionally pause, dipping their slender tongues into the water. It was enchanting.

The deeper she went into the garden, the more Lucy realized that this place felt alive—not just with butterflies, but with the love and kindness that seemed to fill every petal, leaf, and blade of grass. She felt safe and loved, as if the garden were welcoming her into a warm embrace. It was as if the garden itself was whispering secrets to her, secrets about the beauty of nature, the importance of each tiny creature, and the magic that existed all around her.

Then she noticed something incredible: there were caterpillars, some green, some with bright stripes, munching on leaves without a care in the world. She knelt down to watch them, fascinated by their tiny mouths and the way they wiggled as they moved from leaf to leaf. She understood, somehow, that these caterpillars were part of the garden's life cycle, that one day they too would become butterflies and join in the dance around her.

As Lucy continued walking, she came upon a tiny, clear cocoon hanging from a branch. She held her breath, captivated by the delicate casing. It looked like a little house, shining in the light, and she felt a sense of anticipation, as if she were witnessing something special. It struck her that the cocoon was waiting for its own magic to happen, for the caterpillar inside to transform and emerge as a butterfly.

Lucy wandered deeper into her dream garden, observing the butterflies with wide, sparkling eyes, her heart swelling with a feeling she couldn't quite describe. It was more than happiness—it was a connection, a bond with the world around her, like she was a part of something much bigger than herself.

Then, in the distance, she saw something glimmering. It was a small, clear pool, its surface as smooth as glass. Drawn to it, she walked over, her footsteps silent on the soft grass. When she looked down into the water, she gasped. Reflected back at her was the garden, but it looked even more vivid and alive, as if the flowers were leaning closer, and the butterflies were brighter than ever.

But there was something different about her reflection. Her cheeks were flushed, her eyes bright, and there was a glint of excitement in her gaze that made her seem almost as magical as the garden itself. She felt a strange, warm sensation in her heart, a sense that she was exactly where she was meant to be. In that moment, Lucy knew that this dream wasn't just about butterflies and flowers—it was about finding something that made her heart soar.

Then, almost as if the garden could read her thoughts, a breeze began to blow, carrying with it the soft sounds of fluttering wings and the gentle rustle of leaves. The butterflies danced around her, forming a circle as they floated gracefully through the air, their colors blending into a kaleidoscope of hues. Lucy closed her eyes, letting the sounds and scents of the garden fill her senses, feeling a deep peace wash over her.

And then, slowly, the garden began to fade. The colors softened, the butterflies drifted away, and the flowers grew dimmer, like a painting slipping from her grasp. Lucy tried to reach out, to hold onto the beauty around her, but the dream slipped through her fingers like sand.

When she opened her eyes, she was back in her bed, sunlight streaming through her window and casting a warm glow across her room. For a moment, she lay still, blinking as she tried to hold onto the feeling from her dream. She could still picture the butterflies, feel the softness of the petals, and hear the gentle hum of the garden. She even felt a faint warmth in her hand, as if the butterfly she'd held was still resting there.

Sitting up, Lucy looked around her room, still feeling the magic of the dream. She knew it was just a dream, but it felt so real, so vivid, that she couldn't shake the feeling that it meant something special. She looked out her window at her own backyard, with its patches of grass and a few flowers, and felt a small spark of excitement.

Lucy slipped out of bed, tiptoeing to the window. Her backyard looked so ordinary, but she could almost imagine what it might look like filled with flowers, a place where butterflies would want to visit. The idea made her heart beat a little faster. What if, just maybe, she could create a garden like the one in her dream? A place for butterflies, where magic felt real?

The thought made her smile, and she knew, right then, that she couldn't let go of the dream. She didn't tell her parents about it, didn't share it with anyone. Instead, she held it close, letting the feeling grow in her heart like a tiny seed.

As she watched the sunlight dance across her backyard, Lucy whispered to herself, "One day, I'll make a place for you all to come and dance."

And with that, the idea for Lucy's butterfly garden was born.

Chapter 2: The Big Idea

The morning sun streamed through Lucy's window as she woke up, still feeling the magic of her dream garden. She stretched and smiled, her heart racing as the memory of her dream flooded back—the fluttering wings, the bright flowers, and the feeling of being surrounded by so many beautiful butterflies. The dream had felt so real, and the idea of creating her own butterfly garden seemed more exciting than anything she'd ever imagined.

Lucy rushed downstairs, practically skipping with excitement, and found her parents in the kitchen. Her mom was flipping pancakes, and her dad was reading the newspaper. They looked up as she entered, both smiling at her bright expression.

"Good morning, Lucy!" her dad said, putting down his paper. "You seem excited about something."

Lucy took a deep breath, her heart pounding as she tried to put her thoughts into words. "Mom, Dad, I had the most amazing dream last night," she began, her voice filled with wonder. "It was this magical garden, with all these flowers and butterflies everywhere! They were so colorful, and they were flying around me like I was part of their world. It was... it was perfect." She paused, trying to find the right words. "And when I woke up, I thought... what if I could make a real butterfly garden? Right here in our backyard?"

Her parents exchanged a look, clearly surprised but intrigued by her idea. Her mom set down the pancake spatula, smiling warmly. "A butterfly garden?" she asked. "That sounds beautiful, Lucy. But do you know what you'd need to get started?"

Lucy's eyes sparkled as she nodded, her excitement growing. "Well, not exactly," she admitted. "But that's why I was thinking... maybe I could go to the library tomorrow and find some books about butterflies and gardens. I could learn what kinds of flowers they like and what it takes to make a garden that attracts them."

Her dad raised an eyebrow, clearly impressed by her determination. "Going to the library to do research sounds like a smart start," he agreed. "And I think it's a wonderful idea, Lucy. But it'll be a lot of work, you know. Gardens don't just grow overnight."

Lucy nodded eagerly. "I know it'll take time, but I want to learn everything I can. I want to make a place where butterflies feel safe and happy, just like in my dream."

Her mom looked thoughtful, a smile forming on her lips. "Well, I think going to the library is a great plan. You can look up what flowers butterflies love and maybe learn about how to take care of the plants too. And if you need any help, your dad and I will be here for you."

Lucy grinned from ear to ear, her heart soaring with excitement. Her parents thought her idea was good! They believed she could make it happen, and now her dream felt more real than ever. She could already picture herself digging in the garden, planting flowers, and watching butterflies flutter around her.

"Thank you!" she said, bouncing a little in her seat. "Tomorrow, I'll go to the library first thing. I'll borrow as many books as I can carry and start planning everything."

Her dad chuckled, patting her on the back. "That's the spirit. I have a feeling your butterfly garden is going to be something really special, Lucy."

For the rest of the day, Lucy couldn't stop thinking about her butterfly garden. She went outside to her backyard, her eyes scanning the area as she tried to imagine where she'd plant the flowers. She thought about all the colors and types of blooms she could plant, wondering if she'd have room for a small path or a few stones where the butterflies could rest. She wanted it to be perfect—a place that would look and feel like the garden in her dream.

Lucy wandered around the yard, studying the sunlight and shadows. She found a sunny spot where she thought the butterflies would love to warm themselves, a cozy corner where she could plant tall flowers for shelter, and a place in the middle for a cluster of bright, nectar-rich blooms that would draw butterflies in from afar. She made a mental note of it all, feeling like a gardener already.

That evening, Lucy sat on her bed with a notebook, jotting down her ideas and sketching rough plans for the garden. She wrote down words like "colorful flowers," "sunlight," and "safe spaces," trying to capture the feeling of her dream garden on paper. She knew she still had a lot to learn, but the simple act of planning made her feel closer to her goal.

She even wrote a list of questions she wanted to answer when she went to the library. "What kinds of flowers do butterflies like best?" she wrote. "How do you take care of a garden?" and "What other insects are good for a butterfly garden?" She wanted to be prepared so she could start on her garden as soon as possible.

Her mom peeked into her room and saw her writing furiously in her notebook. "Looks like you're already hard at work," she said, smiling.

Lucy looked up, grinning. "I'm making a plan so I don't forget anything! I want to make sure I know exactly what to do when I start planting."

Her mom came over, sitting beside her on the bed. "You're really putting your heart into this, aren't you?" she said softly.

Lucy nodded, her expression serious. "I want it to be just right, Mom. I want the butterflies to feel as welcome as they did in my dream."

Her mom put a hand on her shoulder, a warm look in her eyes. "Well, I think you're already on the right track. Tomorrow, when you go to the library, I'm sure you'll find all the answers you're looking for."

Lucy went to sleep that night with her notebook beside her, feeling hopeful and excited. She could hardly wait for the next day when she'd finally get to the library to learn everything she could about butterflies and gardens.

The following morning, she woke up with the same eagerness, ready to dive into her research. The dream still lingered in her mind, but now it was starting to take shape as something she could make real. Her butterfly garden was no longer just a dream—it was an idea, a goal, and a plan. And with every step, Lucy felt a little closer to bringing her magical garden to life.

Chapter 3: Butterfly Research

The next day, Lucy could hardly contain her excitement. As soon as breakfast was finished, she grabbed her notebook and headed out the door with her mom to the library. Her mom smiled as they walked, clearly amused by Lucy's enthusiasm. Lucy couldn't remember the last time she felt this eager to learn about something—she felt like a young explorer on the edge of a great discovery.

When they arrived at the library, the familiar smell of books and the quiet hum of people reading filled the air. Lucy's mom gave her a gentle nudge. "Go on, Lucy. The gardening and nature section should have everything you need."

Lucy nodded, her heart beating fast as she hurried toward the section her mom pointed out. The shelves stretched high, filled with books on plants, trees, birds, and—finally—butterflies and flowers. Lucy took a deep breath and started scanning the shelves, her eyes wide with wonder. She felt as though each book held a new secret, a new piece of information that would bring her closer to her dream garden.

Her fingers paused on a book titled Butterflies and How to Attract Them, and she carefully pulled it from the shelf. The cover was decorated with bright images of butterflies, and inside were beautiful photos of gardens filled with colorful flowers. She flipped through the pages, her eyes lighting up as she saw names of flowers she'd never heard of before, like "zinnias," "marigolds," and "lantanas." She read that these were "nectar-rich" flowers, which meant they were especially attractive to butterflies.

She jotted down the flower names in her notebook, carefully printing each one. She wanted to make sure she had a variety of plants in her garden to make it colorful and inviting.

Lucy turned to another chapter called "Host Plants for Caterpillars," and her eyes widened with interest. She learned that butterflies lay their eggs on specific plants, where caterpillars can feed as they grow. She read that monarch butterflies, for example, loved milkweed, while swallowtails preferred parsley and dill. She quickly added these plants to her list, realizing that her garden wouldn't just be for butterflies—it could also be a safe place for caterpillars to grow and transform.

With each new fact she learned, Lucy felt her dream garden becoming more real. She imagined a patch of milkweed for the monarchs, some parsley tucked in between the flowers for the swallowtails, and maybe even a few bright marigolds and zinnias to attract butterflies from far and wide.

After a while, Lucy spotted a book titled Gardening for Kids and opened it eagerly. Inside, there were step-by-step guides on planting and taking care of flowers, tips for creating little "butterfly puddling" spots, and even advice on which tools were best for young gardeners. Lucy learned that butterflies loved shallow puddles of water where they could drink and get important nutrients from the soil.

"Shallow puddles," she muttered to herself as she scribbled in her notebook. "I could make a tiny puddle with rocks around it."

She felt a surge of excitement—her garden would be more than just flowers; it would be a real butterfly habitat, complete with flowers for nectar, plants for caterpillars, and a small puddling spot. Lucy could almost picture it, a little corner of the yard bursting with color and life, a place where butterflies could feel at home.

Just as she was about to grab another book, the librarian, an elderly woman with kind eyes, approached her and smiled. "It looks like you're doing some serious research, young lady," she said warmly.

Lucy nodded, grinning. "I'm planning to make a butterfly garden in my backyard, so I'm learning all I can about what butterflies like."

The librarian's eyes lit up. "Well, that sounds wonderful! Butterflies are such special creatures. Did you know they're important pollinators too? Your garden will not only be beautiful, but it will help all the plants around you grow stronger."

Lucy's smile grew even bigger. "I didn't know that! I just wanted to make a place where butterflies would want to visit. But now it sounds like it'll help other things too."

The librarian nodded. "Absolutely. If you need any help finding more information, just let me know. And good luck with your garden! I'm sure it will be lovely."

With the librarian's encouragement, Lucy felt even more inspired. She spent another hour combing through books, adding more notes to her notebook and studying pictures of flowers and butterfly gardens. She learned about planting different flowers that would bloom at different times of the year so her garden would always have something colorful in bloom to attract butterflies. She read that butterflies loved bright colors, especially purples, yellows, and reds, and decided she would make sure to include as many colors as possible.

By the time she finished, her notebook was filled with notes, flower names, planting tips, and a few sketches of how she imagined her garden layout. She felt ready, more than ready, to take the first steps toward creating her butterfly paradise.

As Lucy and her mom checked out her stack of books, her mom looked down at her and smiled. "I'm really proud of you, Lucy. You've put so much effort into this."

Lucy hugged her books close to her chest, beaming. "Thank you, Mom! I can't wait to start planning it all out. I feel like I know exactly what I need to do now."

They headed home, and as soon as they got there, Lucy spread out her books on the kitchen table, opening them to the pages she'd marked. She started organizing her notes, arranging her ideas into categories: nectar flowers, host plants for caterpillars, puddling spots, and garden layout ideas.

She sketched a rough map of her backyard in her notebook, marking where she thought each flower would go. The milkweed would be in a sunny corner, while the parsley and dill could be near the middle, surrounded by colorful flowers like zinnias and marigolds. She added a small circle near the edge labelled "puddle" and sketched little rocks around it, where butterflies could stop for a drink.

Lucy worked late into the afternoon, fine-tuning her plan until she felt it was just right. She went to bed that night with her notebook beside her, feeling a deep sense of satisfaction. She knew there would be hard work ahead—digging, planting, and taking care of the garden every day—but she felt ready for it.

As she drifted off to sleep, she imagined the day her garden would be complete, with bright blooms swaying in the breeze and butterflies fluttering around her. She pictured herself sitting in her butterfly garden, watching as her winged friends danced from flower to flower, each one a reminder of the magical dream that had started it all.

The next steps were clear: she would need to gather her supplies, get the soil ready, and begin planting her flowers. And as Lucy fell asleep, she knew that each day would bring her closer to making her dream garden a reality.

Chapter 4: Gathering Supplies

The morning sunlight filled Lucy's room as she woke up, excitement bubbling up inside her. Today was the day she would gather everything she needed to start her butterfly garden. She rolled out of bed, grabbed her notebook, and flipped to the page where she'd carefully listed all the flowers, plants, and tools she'd need. The words "nectar flowers," "host plants," and "puddling spot" were neatly underlined, each one a crucial part of her plan.

She went downstairs, notebook in hand, and found her mom finishing her coffee at the kitchen table.

"Mom, can we go to the garden store today? I made a list of everything I need for the butterfly garden," Lucy said, practically bouncing in place.

Her mom smiled and nodded. "Of course, Lucy! I'd love to go with you. Let's take a look at your list so we can be sure to get everything you need."

Lucy opened her notebook, showing her mom the careful notes and sketches she'd made from her research at the library. Her list was divided into sections:

1. Nectar Flowers
Zinnias
Marigolds
Lantanas
Coneflowers
2. Host Plants for Caterpillars
Milkweed (for monarchs)
Parsley and dill (for swallowtails)
3. Additional Items
Small stones (for the puddling spot)
Plant markers
Garden gloves

Watering can

Her mom looked over the list, nodding with approval. "You've really thought of everything, Lucy. I'm impressed. It sounds like your garden is going to be amazing!"

Lucy beamed with pride. She could already picture the garden taking shape, each plant playing a special role in welcoming butterflies. "Thank you! I made sure to include everything butterflies like, even a puddling spot where they can drink water."

With the list ready and the plan set, Lucy and her mom climbed into the car and headed to the local garden store. The drive felt longer than usual, and Lucy could hardly sit still, thinking about all the flowers and plants she would soon have. She imagined rows of colorful blooms, and butterflies floating above them, just like in her dream.

When they finally arrived, Lucy's eyes widened at the sight of the garden store. Rows of flowers stretched out as far as she could see, each one bursting with color and fragrance. She grabbed a small cart and pushed it eagerly, leading the way through the aisles.

She started with the flowers, carefully inspecting each plant to make sure it was just right. She chose a few pots of bright zinnias, with petals in shades of red, pink, and orange. Next, she picked out marigolds, their yellow and orange blooms looking as cheerful as a summer day. She added a pot of purple coneflowers, which looked elegant with their long, thin petals. Finally, she found some lantanas, their clusters of small flowers creating a rainbow of colors in each bloom.

Lucy placed each pot carefully into the cart, feeling her excitement build as the flowers added up. She could already picture the butterflies hovering over these beautiful blooms, sipping nectar from their petals. It was as if each flower was a step closer to bringing her dream to life.

Next, she moved to the section with plants for caterpillars. She found a small pot of milkweed, and she was thrilled to see tiny buds on it, a sign that it would bloom soon. She knew monarchs would love it.

She also found parsley and dill plants, remembering that swallowtails were particularly fond of them. She added both to her cart, imagining the caterpillars munching away on the leaves, growing bigger and preparing for their own transformations.

With her plants chosen, she and her mom went over to the garden tools. Lucy picked out a pair of small, colorful gardening gloves to protect her hands while planting. She also chose a watering can, a small trowel, and some plant markers to help her keep track of which plants were which. Finally, she found a few small stones that were perfect for creating her puddling spot. She imagined arranging them around a shallow puddle of water, creating a tiny resting place for butterflies.

As they moved through the store, her mom stopped to admire a section of decorative garden items. "Would you like to add anything to make your garden extra special, Lucy?" she asked, gesturing to some small garden ornaments.

Lucy considered this, then spotted a small ceramic butterfly that would fit perfectly among the flowers. "Can we get this?" she asked, holding up the ornament. "I think it would look nice in the garden, and maybe it'll make the butterflies feel even more welcome."

Her mom smiled and added it to the cart. "I think that's a great idea. It'll be a perfect touch."

With their cart filled, they headed to the checkout counter. Lucy watched each item get rung up, feeling a swell of excitement. She couldn't wait to get started, to dig her hands into the dirt, plant each flower, and create the garden she'd dreamed of.

As they loaded the plants and supplies into the car, Lucy felt a deep sense of accomplishment. She'd done her research, made her plan, and now she had everything she needed to bring her butterfly garden to life.

On the ride home, Lucy chattered non-stop about her plans, explaining how she'd plant each flower, where she'd put the milkweed, and how she'd arrange the stones for the puddling spot. Her mom listened with a smile, clearly proud of Lucy's dedication.

When they got home, Lucy carefully unloaded each plant and tool, setting them on the back patio. She arranged the pots in the order she'd plant them, and her notebook lay open beside her with her sketch of the garden layout.

Her mom knelt beside her, looking over her shoulder. "It looks like you're all set, Lucy. Tomorrow, you can start digging and planting."

Lucy nodded, feeling a rush of excitement and a little bit of nervousness. She knew that planting a garden would be hard work, but she was ready for it. Her dream was finally becoming real, and she was determined to make it beautiful.

That night, Lucy lay in bed, imagining her garden. She pictured the zinnias and marigolds stretching toward the sun, the milkweed growing tall and strong, and the butterflies fluttering around her in a colorful dance. She felt a sense of pride and happiness, knowing that her dream garden was no longer just an idea—it was a project, one she'd soon see blooming right before her eyes.

Chapter 5: First Steps in the Garden

The next morning, Lucy woke up early, her heart racing with excitement. Today, she would start creating her butterfly garden. She quickly put on her gardening gloves, grabbed her notebook, and rushed outside, where her dad was already setting up a few tools by the spot they had chosen for the garden. Her mom joined them, carrying a spade and a small rake, ready to help.

Lucy looked around at the area she had mapped out, imagining how it would look filled with colorful flowers and fluttering butterflies. But for now, it was just a bare patch of dirt. She knew, though, that every beautiful garden had to start somewhere, and today was all about the first steps.

Her dad knelt down and showed her the tools they'd need for preparing the soil: a shovel for digging, a rake for smoothing, and a hoe for breaking up any clumps. He handed her the small rake, explaining how it would help her loosen the soil so the roots of her flowers would have room to grow.

"Good soil is the foundation of any garden," her dad explained as he dug into the earth. "If the soil is too hard, the roots can't grow deep, and the plants won't be as strong."

Lucy watched as her dad demonstrated, carefully loosening and turning the soil. She took her small rake and began digging into the ground, pulling the dirt apart just like her dad had shown her. The soil was crumbly and cool under her fingers, and she was surprised at how satisfying it felt to break it up.

"This is hard work," she said, laughing as she wiped a bit of dirt from her forehead. "But I want the butterflies to have a good home, so I'll make sure it's perfect."

Her mom smiled and handed her a small bag. "We can also add some compost to the soil. It's full of nutrients that will help your flowers grow strong and healthy, which will make them extra attractive to butterflies."

Lucy opened the bag and sprinkled some compost over the loosened soil, her nose wrinkling slightly at its earthy smell. She worked it into the dirt, mixing it as best as she could, knowing it would be worth it once the flowers started to bloom.

After a while, Lucy's dad took the shovel and began digging deeper in a few spots, explaining that some plants would need a little extra depth for their roots. Lucy listened carefully, fascinated by how much thought went into something as simple as soil. She had never realized that plants needed so much more than just a place to sit—they needed a foundation that would give them strength to grow tall and healthy.

As they worked, her mom pointed out small creatures wriggling in the soil. "Look, Lucy, these are earthworms! They're actually really good for the garden."

Lucy knelt down to get a closer look at the worms. "How do they help?"

"They dig through the soil, creating little tunnels that help air and water reach the roots of plants," her mom explained. "Plus, as they eat, they leave behind nutrients that help plants grow."

Lucy smiled at the thought of having helpful little worms in her garden. "Thanks for helping, little guys," she whispered to them, imagining that they were already part of her garden team.

For the next few hours, Lucy, her mom, and her dad worked together, digging, loosening, and enriching the soil. They took breaks to sip cool lemonade and rest in the shade, but Lucy always bounced back up, eager to keep going. The patch of dirt slowly transformed into a soft, rich bed, ready for planting.

Finally, when the soil was just right, Lucy and her family stood back to admire their work. Her hands and face were smudged with dirt, and she was a little tired, but she felt a deep sense of pride. This soil, which had once been hard and rough, was now a perfect foundation for her butterfly garden.

Her dad clapped her on the shoulder. "Great job, Lucy. This is going to be a fantastic garden. And because you prepared the soil so well, your flowers will have everything they need to grow big and beautiful."

Lucy nodded, feeling a rush of excitement as she looked over the rich, dark soil. Her plants were going to have the best start she could give them, and she could hardly wait to see them take root and bloom. She felt a new appreciation for all the work that went into making a garden, understanding now that a strong beginning was essential for her dream to come to life.

That night, as Lucy washed up, she felt a pleasant ache in her muscles, a reminder of the hard work she'd put into her garden that day. She thought about the soil, rich and ready, and the tiny earthworms already helping her garden. She went to bed feeling proud and eager, knowing that tomorrow, she'd take the next step in her garden journey: planting the flowers she'd carefully chosen to bring the butterflies to her yard.

As she drifted off to sleep, she could almost see her garden growing before her eyes. The zinnias, marigolds, milkweed, and coneflowers would soon be stretching toward the sun, rooted deeply in the soil she'd prepared with so much care. And just like her dream, butterflies would soon be gliding through her garden, resting on the flowers that were only beginning to sprout from her first steps.

Chapter 6: The Seed Planting Party

Lucy could hardly wait to start planting, but she had an even better idea in mind. Instead of planting the seeds by herself, she decided it would be fun to invite her friends over to help. After all, a butterfly garden was meant to be shared, and it would be even more special if her friends were part of the creation.

That afternoon, she called her friends Mia, Ben, and Sophia, inviting them to come over the next day to help plant the seeds. She explained her plan to create a butterfly garden, and her excitement was contagious. They all agreed enthusiastically, promising to bring their gardening gloves and, most importantly, their excitement.

The next day was sunny and warm—the perfect day for a planting party. Lucy had set everything up in the backyard, organizing the seeds, small trowels, watering cans, and even a few extra gardening gloves. She'd also prepared a table with lemonade, cookies, and a bright bouquet of flowers she'd picked from her mom's flower bed to make the setting extra cheerful.

When her friends arrived, Lucy welcomed them with a big smile. "Thank you all so much for coming! Today, we're planting seeds for my butterfly garden. I thought it would be fun if we all helped—then, when the flowers bloom and the butterflies come, it'll be like our special garden."

Mia, Ben, and Sophia looked around with wide eyes, clearly excited about the project. Ben picked up one of the seed packets, reading the label. "Coneflowers! My mom has these in her garden, and they're so pretty."

Mia grinned, grabbing a small trowel. "I've never planted anything before, but I'm ready to learn!"

Lucy clapped her hands, thrilled that her friends were as excited as she was. "Great! Let's get started!"

She showed them how to use the trowels to dig small holes, explaining that each flower needed its own space to grow. She handed out seed packets—zinnias, marigolds, milkweed, and coneflowers—and explained which areas they'd mapped out for each type. Lucy remembered what she'd learned about where each flower would get the best sunlight and grow best.

Together, they worked side by side, digging small holes and carefully dropping the seeds in, covering them with soil and patting it down gently. Mia giggled as she sprinkled marigold seeds into her spot, trying to be as precise as possible.

Ben looked up from his coneflower patch. "Lucy, how did you come up with the idea for a butterfly garden?"

Lucy paused, her face lighting up as she remembered her dream. "I had this magical dream about a garden full of butterflies. It was so beautiful that I wanted to make it real. I thought if I planted the right flowers, butterflies would come, and we'd have a real garden just like the one in my dream."

Sophia smiled, planting some milkweed. "That's such a sweet idea, Lucy. I think it's already starting to feel magical."

They all worked together, taking turns watering each section after planting. The soil darkened under the water, and the scent of damp earth filled the air. Lucy showed her friends how to be gentle with the watering cans, making sure not to flood the seeds.

As they planted, they talked and laughed, sharing stories about butterflies they'd seen in their own yards. Mia told them about a bright yellow butterfly that had landed on her bike handle, while Ben shared how he once saw a butterfly resting on his window. Sophia promised to keep an eye out for any butterflies in her neighbourhood, knowing that someday soon, they'd have a garden filled with them.

Once they'd finished planting, they stood back to admire their work. The garden patch was still mostly soil, but they could all imagine the flowers that would soon bloom there. Lucy felt a deep sense of happiness as she looked around at her friends, each of them smiling and proud of what they'd created together.

"Thank you so much, everyone," she said, her voice filled with gratitude. "When the butterflies come, it'll be because of all of us."

Her friends beamed, each one clearly proud to have played a part in the garden. Lucy poured lemonade for everyone, and they sat together, enjoying their drinks and admiring the garden plot that now held their hopes and hard work. As they sat, they began talking about what the garden would look like in a few weeks, and they made plans to come back together to check on the flowers' progress.

Mia pointed to a small rock near the edge of the garden. "We should paint some rocks and put them around the garden," she suggested. "Maybe with butterfly designs or little words like 'Welcome' and 'Grow.'"

Ben nodded enthusiastically. "Yeah, that would look awesome! We could each paint one and bring it next time."

Lucy loved the idea. "Let's do it! Next time we meet, we'll paint rocks for the garden. It'll make it feel even more like ours."

They finished their lemonade, and as the sun began to dip lower in the sky, her friends said their goodbyes, each one promising to visit the garden soon to see how it was coming along.

As Lucy watched them leave, she felt an overwhelming sense of happiness. Her butterfly garden was no longer just her project; it was now something she shared with the people she cared about. It was a place where her friends' laughter and hard work were mixed with the soil, ready to bring the garden to life.

That night, as Lucy lay in bed, she felt a warm glow in her heart. She imagined each seed sprouting, reaching toward the sun, and eventually blossoming into colorful flowers that would welcome butterflies from near and far. And when they arrived, those butterflies would be fluttering over a garden that wasn't just hers, but a place of shared joy and teamwork.

Her dream garden was no longer just an idea; it was a true community project. With the help of her friends, she was one step closer to bringing her magical vision to life.

Chapter 7: Watering and Waiting

After the excitement of the Seed Planting Party, Lucy woke up each morning with a single thought: I wonder if anything has started to grow. She'd quickly slip on her gardening gloves, grab her little watering can, and rush outside to check on her butterfly garden.

The garden patch was still mostly bare soil, with no hint of the colorful flowers she imagined in her mind. But Lucy remembered what her parents had told her about gardens needing time, care, and patience. So, she carefully sprinkled water over each area, making sure not to drench the soil but just give it a light, even misting.

As the days went by, watering became her special morning routine. She loved the sound of the water splashing onto the soil, the scent of the fresh earth, and the anticipation that maybe, just maybe, a green sprout would poke through the soil that day. Each morning, she'd kneel down, her eyes scanning the dirt, hoping to see the first sign of life.

One morning, after nearly a week of watering, Lucy was sitting on her knees, examining the soil. "Come on, little seeds," she whispered with a smile. "I know you can do it. Just keep growing a little more every day."

Her dad came over, watching her as she crouched near the garden, her face full of concentration and hope. "You're taking good care of them, Lucy," he said with a smile. "But remember, gardens need time. Plants grow slowly, little by little. Sometimes, you can't see any changes, but a lot is happening underground."

Lucy looked up, her face thoughtful. "You mean, even if I can't see anything yet, they're still working on growing?"

He nodded. "Exactly. Those roots are growing deeper, getting ready to support strong flowers. It's like how we can't build a tall house without a good foundation. It's all part of the process."

Lucy smiled, feeling a bit reassured. It was kind of like a hidden secret—something she couldn't see yet, but knew was happening beneath the surface. "So, the seeds are taking their time getting ready to bloom?"

"That's right," her dad replied. "And just like us, they need water, sunlight, and patience."

Lucy kept these words in mind, reminding herself each day that her plants were growing in ways she couldn't yet see. She watered the soil gently each morning and spent her afternoons reading her gardening books or chatting with her friends about the garden. Ben, Mia, and Sophia were all eager for updates, and Lucy would proudly tell them about how the soil was staying moist and healthy. They'd giggle and joke, calling her the "Garden Guardian."

Then, one morning, after days of watering and waiting, Lucy spotted something small and green poking out of the soil. Her heart skipped a beat as she knelt down to examine it closely. It was a tiny sprout, barely an inch tall, with two tiny leaves reaching for the sunlight. She gasped in excitement and called for her mom and dad, who quickly came over.

"Look! A sprout!" she exclaimed, her voice filled with pride. "It's really growing!"

Her mom smiled, kneeling beside her. "See? All your hard work is paying off, Lucy. This little sprout is the first of many."

Lucy gently touched the little plant, marveling at how delicate it looked yet feeling proud of the strength it represented. It was the first visible sign of all the effort she'd put in, and it made her heart swell with happiness.

Over the next few days, more sprouts began to appear. Each morning, Lucy would discover another tiny shoot poking up through the soil, like little green flags waving in celebration. She continued her watering routine, careful not to overdo it, and watched in amazement as each sprout grew a little taller, their leaves unfurling like tiny hands reaching up to the sun.

One day, as she watered her garden, Lucy thought about how much she'd learned in the past few weeks. Waiting for her flowers to grow was like waiting for a surprise—you couldn't rush it, but when it happened, it was worth every second of patience.

Every morning, she checked on the sprouts, feeling more and more grateful for the time she spent caring for them. The excitement she felt was different from the rush of starting something new; it was deeper, more satisfying. She realized that sometimes, the best things took time, and the waiting made the reward even sweeter.

On a particularly warm afternoon, Mia, Ben, and Sophia came over to see the garden. Lucy proudly showed them the sprouts, each one a testament to her dedication and patience.

"They're really growing!" Mia said, bending down to get a closer look. "They look so healthy!"

Lucy nodded, her face beaming with pride. "It's all thanks to the watering and waiting. I had to be patient, but it was totally worth it."

Ben grinned. "I can't wait until they're all flowers! I bet the butterflies will love it here."

Lucy couldn't wait either. As she watched her friends marvel at the sprouts, she felt a new appreciation for each little green leaf. These sprouts were only the beginning, but they held the promise of the beautiful butterfly garden she'd dreamed of. And she knew that as long as she kept watering, waiting, and caring for them, her garden would grow into something magical.

Each day, Lucy continued her routine, feeling her patience grow along with the plants. It wasn't easy waiting, but every new leaf and every inch of growth was a reminder that her dream garden was slowly, but surely, becoming real. And when the day finally came for the flowers to bloom, she knew it would be even more special, thanks to all the watering, waiting, and love she'd put into it.

As she lay in bed that night, Lucy felt peaceful and happy, knowing she was learning one of the most important lessons a gardener could learn: the beauty of patience. And in her heart, she knew that just like her flowers, her garden of dreams was growing right along with each tiny sprout.

Chapter 8: The First Sprouts

The days of watering and waiting were finally paying off. One bright morning, Lucy slipped on her gardening gloves, grabbed her little watering can, and hurried outside, just as she did every day. But today, something was different. As she approached her butterfly garden, her eyes widened in surprise and excitement.

The tiny sprouts that had poked up just a week ago were no longer small and delicate. They were growing taller, with sturdy little stems and more leaves reaching for the sunlight. Each sprout looked bigger, stronger, and full of life. Lucy could hardly believe how much they'd grown in just a few days. Her dream garden was starting to come alive, and her heart filled with a mix of joy and pride.

"Mom! Dad! Come see!" she called, unable to contain her excitement.

Her parents stepped outside and joined her in the garden, both of them smiling as they saw the transformation. Her mom knelt down, carefully inspecting the sprouts with admiration. "Look at that, Lucy! They're really taking off. All your hard work is paying off."

Lucy beamed. "They're getting so big! I can almost imagine the flowers blooming already."

Her dad chuckled. "That's the magic of patience and care. These sprouts are growing strong because you gave them everything they needed."

Lucy crouched beside her garden, admiring each sprout and gently brushing her fingers over the leaves. They felt soft and cool, like tiny promises of the flowers to come. She could picture the zinnias, marigolds, milkweed, and coneflowers that would eventually blossom, each one inviting butterflies to visit. Her excitement grew as she imagined the first butterfly landing on a petal.

Every morning after that, Lucy rushed outside to check on her garden. Each day, she noticed something new: more leaves, taller stems, and even the beginnings of small buds on some of the plants. Her friends were just as excited as she was. When Mia, Ben, and Sophia came over, they marvelled at the growth, and Lucy could tell they were proud to have been part of the planting process.

"They're getting so big!" Mia exclaimed, gently touching a leaf. "I can't believe how much they've grown!"

"Pretty soon, we'll have flowers," Ben added, his face lighting up. "I can already imagine all the butterflies we'll see."

Sophia nodded, grinning. "I think it'll be even more beautiful than we imagined. You did an amazing job, Lucy."

Lucy felt a swell of happiness as she listened to her friends. The garden wasn't just hers—it was theirs, a little corner of the world they'd all helped bring to life. She felt proud, not just of the plants but of all the time, love, and patience that had gone into every step.

Over the next few days, the buds continued to grow, swelling with promise. Lucy would run her fingers gently over them, almost as if she could encourage them to bloom with just a touch. She watched them carefully, her heart filled with anticipation as the buds slowly opened, revealing tiny flashes of color beneath the green.

One morning, as she stepped outside, her breath caught. The first zinnia had bloomed. It was a vivid pink, its petals unfurling like a small, vibrant sunrise in her garden. She knelt down, unable to take her eyes off the flower. It was more beautiful than she'd imagined, its color bright and inviting, as if it were calling to butterflies to come and visit.

"Mom, Dad!" she shouted, barely able to contain herself. Her parents came rushing over, smiling as they saw the bloom.

Her mom placed a gentle hand on her shoulder. "It's beautiful, Lucy. The first flower of your butterfly garden."

Her dad nodded. "And there will be plenty more to come. You've created a garden that's ready to welcome all kinds of visitors."

Lucy felt a surge of pride as she looked at the flower, her heart filled with wonder. This wasn't just a flower; it was the result of all her care, her patience, and her dream. And as she looked closer, she spotted something even more magical: a small butterfly, flitting around the garden as if it had been drawn by the bright new bloom.

The butterfly was small, with delicate blue and black wings, and it fluttered around the zinnia before settling gently on one of its petals. Lucy held her breath, afraid to move and disturb the tiny creature. She felt like she was back in her dream, standing in a magical garden surrounded by butterflies.

As the butterfly drank from the flower, Lucy's friends arrived, their eyes widening as they saw the new bloom and the butterfly visitor. They tiptoed over, each of them gazing at the butterfly in awe.

"Lucy, it's happening!" Mia whispered, her voice filled with excitement. "The butterflies are coming!"

Lucy could hardly believe it herself. Her garden, the one she'd dreamed of and nurtured from the very beginning, was now alive with color, beauty, and life. The flowers were growing big and strong, and the butterflies were arriving, just as she'd hoped.

As the days went by, more flowers began to bloom, each one adding its own splash of color to the garden. Yellow marigolds, purple coneflowers, and orange milkweed blossoms began to open, creating a beautiful, colorful display. And with each new flower, more butterflies came—delicate monarchs, tiny blues, and even a few bright yellow swallowtails. The garden was alive, a haven for butterflies, just as Lucy had imagined.

Every morning, Lucy would sit by her garden, watching her flowers sway in the breeze and the butterflies dance from bloom to bloom. She felt proud of what she'd created, and every butterfly that fluttered by felt like a special thank you.

As she watched her garden, Lucy realized that all the watering, waiting, and work had been worth it. She'd learned that patience could bring about the most beautiful things, and that sometimes, the most magical moments came from dreams you worked hard to make real.

And now, surrounded by her friends and her blooming butterfly garden, Lucy knew she'd created something truly special—something she'd cherish forever.

Chapter 9: The Pests Arrive

Lucy's garden was in full bloom, with flowers in every color and butterflies visiting daily. Her dream was finally coming to life, and she loved nothing more than spending her mornings watching butterflies flutter from flower to flower. But one day, as she bent down to admire her zinnias, she noticed something strange. Tiny holes dotted the leaves, and some plants looked a bit wilted.

Her heart sank as she inspected her garden more closely. She found small, green bugs crawling on some leaves, and a few caterpillars that didn't look like the butterflies she'd hoped to attract. Her beautiful plants, the ones she and her friends had worked so hard to grow, were being munched on by pests!

Lucy ran inside to find her mom, who was washing dishes in the kitchen. "Mom! There are bugs eating my plants! What should I do?" she asked, worry etched across her face.

Her mom dried her hands and gave her a reassuring smile. "Let's go take a look," she said. Together, they walked back to the garden, and Lucy pointed out the little green bugs and the holes they'd left behind.

Her mom knelt down, examining the plants. "It looks like you have a few garden pests. They're pretty common, especially when plants are so young and fresh. But don't worry—there are ways to keep them away without using anything harmful to the butterflies or your garden."

Lucy felt a small wave of relief. "What can we do to get rid of them without hurting the butterflies?"

Her mom thought for a moment. "One of the best ways is to use natural methods. There are certain plants and creatures that can help protect your garden without using any chemicals. How about we go to the library and see what we can find?"

Excited by the idea of learning more, Lucy quickly agreed. They went to the library that afternoon and found a section on organic gardening. Lucy discovered that there were actually many ways to protect her plants naturally.

She took notes in her notebook as she learned about companion planting—where certain plants help keep pests away from others. She read that marigolds, for example, have a strong scent that can deter many pests, and basil can help keep bugs away from other plants. She'd already planted some marigolds, but she decided she'd add a few more around her garden for extra protection.

Then Lucy found a page about attracting "beneficial insects"—insects that would help protect her plants by eating the pests. Ladybugs, she read, were natural predators of aphids, the little green bugs she'd seen on her plants. She was fascinated to learn that ladybugs were actually helpful and could act as tiny guardians for her garden.

Armed with new knowledge, Lucy returned home with her mom and set to work. First, she carefully planted more marigolds around her garden, spacing them between her zinnias, coneflowers, and milkweed. As she pressed the marigold seeds into the soil, she whispered, "Keep the bad bugs away, please."

The next day, Lucy and her dad went to the local garden store, where they found a small container of ladybugs. She couldn't believe she could actually buy ladybugs to release into her garden! The store owner explained that ladybugs would settle in her garden, eating aphids and other harmful pests while leaving her flowers and butterflies alone.

Lucy was thrilled as they headed home, carefully holding the container of ladybugs in her hands. When she got to the garden, she carefully opened the container and watched in wonder as the little red and black-spotted beetles crawled out, exploring her flowers and leaves.

"Go ahead, little friends," she whispered. "Make yourselves at home."

Over the next few days, Lucy noticed a difference. The aphids and other pests seemed to be disappearing, and her flowers looked healthier and happier. She spotted the ladybugs on her plants, munching away on the pests, just as the library books had said they would. She loved knowing that her garden now had its own little team of helpers, keeping it safe and healthy.

One morning, while watering her plants, Lucy noticed that the leaves looked fresh and strong again, with fewer holes and no sign of the aphids. Her flowers were back to blooming beautifully, and her butterfly visitors returned, flitting happily from flower to flower.

Mia, Ben, and Sophia came over later that day to check on the garden, and Lucy proudly showed them the marigolds she'd planted as natural protectors. She also pointed out a ladybug resting on a milkweed leaf.

"Did you know ladybugs eat the pests that were hurting my plants?" she asked, a proud smile on her face.

Ben's eyes widened in surprise. "I didn't know that! So, they're like little garden warriors?"

"Exactly!" Lucy replied, nodding. "They protect the plants without hurting the butterflies or the flowers."

Sophia grinned as she gently touched a marigold leaf. "That's so cool! You learned all this from the library?"

Lucy nodded. "Yep! There are so many natural ways to take care of a garden. I wanted to make sure the butterflies were safe, so I looked for ways to keep the pests away without using anything harmful."

Her friends admired the garden, impressed by her efforts. Lucy felt proud of how much she'd learned and how she'd managed to protect her garden naturally. It felt good to know that her flowers could bloom freely and that her butterfly visitors would stay safe and happy.

As she watered her garden later that day, Lucy felt a deep sense of peace. She realized that gardening wasn't just about planting seeds and watching them grow. It was about taking care of each flower, each leaf, and creating a safe, welcoming space for every creature, big and small.

Lucy whispered to her garden, "Thank you, little ladybugs and marigolds, for helping me keep this garden safe." She knew she still had more to learn, but she was ready for it. Her butterfly garden was becoming more than just a dream; it was a living, breathing space, filled with life, color, and the gentle care she'd given it.

With each new bloom, Lucy's garden continued to grow, a place of beauty, protection, and harmony, ready to welcome every butterfly that fluttered by.

Chapter 10: A Little Help from Ladybugs

Lucy's garden was blooming beautifully, with colorful flowers stretching toward the sun and butterflies visiting each day. Thanks to her marigold "guardians" and the handful of ladybugs she had released, most of the pesky aphids had disappeared. But as her garden grew bigger, so did the need for more helpers to protect it.

One afternoon, as Lucy was inspecting her plants, she noticed a few more aphids creeping up on her zinnias. She frowned, realizing that while her ladybug friends had done a great job, they could use some reinforcements. Determined to keep her flowers safe, Lucy decided it was time to introduce more ladybugs to her garden.

That weekend, she and her dad headed to the garden store again. As soon as she entered, Lucy spotted a little container filled with dozens of tiny ladybugs, each one scurrying around in search of a new home. The sight of so many ladybugs made her smile—she couldn't wait to set them free in her garden.

When they returned home, Lucy carefully brought the container over to her flower patch. She opened the lid slowly, watching as the ladybugs crawled onto her fingers, their tiny legs tickling her skin. She gently transferred them to her flowers, watching as they spread out, each one finding its own place among the leaves and petals.

"Go on, little friends," Lucy said with a smile. "Make yourselves at home and help keep my garden safe."

As the ladybugs explored, Lucy knelt down, mesmerized by how they moved. Some ladybugs immediately found aphids to munch on, while others climbed up the stems, scouting their new territory. She felt a sense of wonder as she watched them work, realizing that these tiny creatures were playing an important role in keeping her plants healthy.

Later that day, her mom joined her in the garden, smiling as she saw the ladybugs scattered across the flowers. "You know, Lucy," her mom said, "ladybugs aren't the only helpers in the garden. There are other insects that work together in nature, each one doing its part to keep plants and flowers safe."

Lucy's eyes widened. "Really? Like who?"

"Well, for one, there are bees," her mom explained, pointing to a bee buzzing around a flower nearby. "They help by pollinating flowers. When they move from one flower to another, they spread pollen, which helps the flowers grow and produce seeds."

Lucy watched the bee as it flew from flower to flower, its tiny legs dusted with pollen. She hadn't thought of bees as garden helpers before, but now she saw how they, too, were part of the garden's team.

"And then there are spiders," her mom continued. "Even though they can be a little creepy, spiders help by catching other pests that might harm the plants."

Lucy scrunched her nose a little but nodded, realizing that every creature had its role, even the ones that weren't as cute as ladybugs. She was beginning to understand that her garden was a little ecosystem, a place where different insects worked together, each one helping in its own way.

Feeling inspired, Lucy decided to observe her garden even more closely. Over the next few days, she kept an eye on the ladybugs, bees, and even the occasional spider, watching how they each played a part in the health of her garden. She noticed that the ladybugs loved munching on aphids, and whenever a bee buzzed by, it always seemed to visit as many flowers as it could.

Her friends, Mia, Ben, and Sophia, stopped by to check on the garden one afternoon, and Lucy couldn't wait to share what she'd learned.

"Did you know ladybugs aren't the only ones helping the garden?" she asked, her eyes lighting up with excitement.

Her friends looked curious. "Who else is helping?" Ben asked, peering into the flowers.

Lucy pointed to a bee hovering over a milkweed flower. "Bees help by pollinating the flowers, which helps them grow strong and make seeds. And even spiders catch pests that might hurt the plants."

Mia watched the bee with a newfound appreciation. "That's so cool! I never knew bugs could work together like that."

Sophia nodded, smiling. "It's like a team, all working together to keep the garden healthy."

Lucy grinned, feeling a deep sense of pride in her garden. She realized that by inviting these little helpers into her garden, she'd created a small world where each creature could thrive and support each other.

Over the next week, Lucy watched as her garden grew stronger and healthier, with fewer signs of pests and more flowers blooming. The ladybugs had settled in, and she often spotted them nestled on leaves or munching on an aphid snack. The bees came every day, too, making their rounds through the flowers, their buzzing becoming a familiar, comforting sound.

One morning, as Lucy was watering her garden, she felt a special connection to her little insect team. Each creature played a unique role, and together, they created a balance that made her garden bloom. She understood now that a garden wasn't just about the flowers or butterflies—it was about creating a place where every small helper could thrive.

Lucy knelt by her flowers, whispering a quiet thank-you to her ladybugs, bees, and even the occasional spider, feeling grateful for their hard work. She'd learned that in nature, every creature has a role, and even the smallest insect could make a big difference.

As she stood up, she looked over her garden with a sense of wonder and pride. Her butterfly garden had grown into a place of color, life, and harmony, a small world where flowers, butterflies, and insects worked together. And as she watched a new ladybug crawl across a petal, she knew that her garden had become exactly what she'd dreamed—a safe, thriving place for all.

Chapter 11: Meeting Mr. Hummingbird

The garden was buzzing with life. Butterflies danced from bloom to bloom, bees hummed around the flowers, and Lucy's little ladybug friends were hard at work keeping the plants safe. But one bright morning, as Lucy was watering her garden, she noticed something fluttering quickly just above her flowers—a flash of shimmering green and red.

Lucy froze, her eyes widening in awe. It was a tiny hummingbird, hovering gracefully near her zinnias. She'd never seen one so close before, and she couldn't believe how small and vibrant it was. Its wings moved so fast they were just a blur, and it seemed to hover effortlessly as it dipped its long, thin beak into a flower.

"Mom! Dad! Come quick!" she whispered excitedly.

Her parents joined her, smiling as they watched the little bird. "Looks like you have a new visitor," her mom said softly.

Lucy couldn't take her eyes off the hummingbird. "It's amazing! It's like it's floating in the air!" she whispered, mesmerized.

Her dad smiled. "That's a hummingbird for you. They're amazing creatures, and they're excellent pollinators, just like bees. They help flowers by spreading pollen as they visit each bloom for nectar."

Lucy watched as the hummingbird moved from flower to flower, its tiny beak dipping into the center of each blossom. She noticed that it seemed to prefer the bright red and orange flowers, spending more time around the zinnias and the marigolds. She felt a wave of excitement, realizing that her garden was attracting even more types of creatures.

"Do they help the flowers grow too?" Lucy asked, glancing up at her dad.

He nodded. "Yes. Just like bees, hummingbirds spread pollen from one flower to another, which helps the flowers produce seeds. They're really helpful in gardens and are especially drawn to red and orange flowers because of the color."

Lucy smiled, feeling even prouder of her garden. She'd read about how to attract butterflies and bees, but now she saw that her garden was drawing in other pollinators too, each one playing a special role.

Over the next few days, Lucy noticed that the hummingbird—whom she decided to call Mr. Hummingbird—returned often, especially during the mornings when the flowers were fresh with morning dew. She loved watching him dart from flower to flower, sometimes so quickly she could barely keep track of where he'd go next.

One day, while she was observing Mr. Hummingbird, her friend Mia came over and noticed Lucy sitting quietly near the garden, her eyes fixed on the flowers.

"What are you looking at?" Mia asked, crouching down beside her.

Lucy grinned and whispered, "Shh! Look, right there, by the zinnias."

Mia followed her gaze, her mouth dropping open as she spotted the hummingbird. "Wow! I've never seen one so close before! He's so tiny—and look at those colors!"

Lucy nodded, keeping her voice low. "His name is Mr. Hummingbird, and he's been visiting the garden every day. He helps spread pollen, just like the bees."

Mia watched in awe as the hummingbird flitted from flower to flower, pausing just long enough to sip nectar before darting to the next bloom. "That's incredible! I didn't know hummingbirds were pollinators too."

Lucy smiled, feeling a surge of pride. "Me neither, but I've learned that every creature has a role in helping the garden. The bees, the ladybugs, the butterflies, and now even Mr. Hummingbird."

As the days went by, Lucy began to understand just how important each visitor was to her garden. The butterflies brought beauty, the bees and hummingbirds helped the flowers grow, and the ladybugs kept pests away. It was as if her garden had its own little community, with each creature working together to keep it healthy and thriving.

One evening, as Lucy sat outside watching her garden, her mom joined her with a cup of tea, sitting down beside her. "Your garden is really something special, Lucy," she said warmly. "You've created a space that's not only beautiful but also full of life."

Lucy nodded, watching as Mr. Hummingbird appeared once again, dipping down to sip from a marigold. "It feels like all the creatures are helping each other. It's like... they're a team," she said thoughtfully.

Her mom smiled, nodding in agreement. "That's exactly right. Nature is full of teams, working together in ways we don't always notice. By creating this garden, you've invited them to join in, and now they're helping you take care of it."

Lucy felt a deep sense of happiness and pride. Her butterfly garden was so much more than flowers and colors—it was a place where life could thrive, where every creature had a purpose. Mr. Hummingbird, the bees, the butterflies, and the ladybugs had all become part of her garden family, each one adding its own special magic.

The next morning, Lucy decided to add a small hummingbird feeder to the garden, filling it with sugar water just like she'd read in her gardening book. She hung it from a low tree branch nearby, hoping it would give Mr. Hummingbird and his friends an extra reason to visit.

Sure enough, within hours, Mr. Hummingbird returned, hovering near the feeder before taking a quick sip. Lucy watched him, feeling a sense of joy in knowing she was giving back to the creatures who helped her garden thrive.

As Lucy stood back to admire her garden, she realized it had become more beautiful than she could have ever imagined. Her dream had come to life, not only with flowers and butterflies but with bees, ladybugs, and even a hummingbird—all working together to create something truly special.

She whispered to herself, "Thank you, Mr. Hummingbird, and thank you, little garden team. You've made my dream garden even better than I could have dreamed."

And as she watched Mr. Hummingbird flutter away, she felt a deep sense of connection to the world around her, grateful for every creature who had found a home in her butterfly garden.

Chapter 12: Naming Her Visitors

Lucy's garden had blossomed into a beautiful, colorful haven, and every day brought new visitors. Butterflies, bees, ladybugs, and Mr. Hummingbird came and went, each one adding a touch of magic to her garden. But the butterflies held a special place in her heart. They were delicate, graceful, and each one seemed to have its own personality.

One morning, as Lucy sat by the garden, a small orange and black butterfly fluttered toward her and landed on a bright zinnia bloom. Lucy watched it closely, admiring the intricate pattern on its wings. It was a monarch butterfly, one she had learned about in her books. She couldn't help but smile as the butterfly lingered on the flower, as if it were saying hello.

"Hello, beautiful one," she whispered. "I think I'll call you... Sunny, because you look like a little piece of sunshine."

The butterfly flitted its wings gently, as if in approval, before floating over to the milkweed. Lucy imagined Sunny had a cheerful personality, always bringing joy to every flower it visited. In her mind, Sunny was like the garden's welcoming committee, inviting other butterflies to come and enjoy the flowers.

From that moment on, Lucy decided she would name each butterfly that visited her garden. Every day brought new faces, and each butterfly had something special about it that inspired a new name and story.

A small blue butterfly with tiny white spots appeared next, hovering over the coneflowers. Lucy thought it looked shy, its delicate wings fluttering softly, almost hesitantly. She named it Sky, imagining it had come from a faraway land in the clouds, only stopping by her garden to rest before continuing on its journey.

"Sky, you're a little explorer, aren't you?" she said, smiling as the butterfly moved gracefully between the flowers.

The next visitor was a bright yellow butterfly that darted quickly from flower to flower, never lingering in one place for long. It seemed energetic and a little mischievous, as if it were playing a game of tag with the other butterflies. Lucy named it Flash, picturing it as the fastest butterfly in the garden, always on the move and ready for a new adventure.

"Flash, you're like a little lightning bolt," she whispered as it zoomed past her, making her giggle.

Each day, Lucy discovered new butterflies, each with a unique pattern or color. She met a small white butterfly with tiny black tips on its wings, which she named Snowy, imagining it had drifted down like a snowflake. Then there was a graceful black butterfly with iridescent blue spots, whom she called Midnight, picturing it flying under the stars, bringing nighttime magic to the garden.

With each new visitor, Lucy created little stories in her mind. Sometimes she'd sit in her garden, talking softly to the butterflies, sharing her stories with them as if they could understand. She imagined that Sunny, Sky, Flash, Snowy, and Midnight each had their own special world they came from, each one bringing a little piece of that world into her garden.

Her friends, Mia, Ben, and Sophia, were fascinated by Lucy's names and stories when they came to visit.

"Look, that's Flash!" Lucy said one afternoon, pointing to the bright yellow butterfly darting around the marigolds. "Flash is the fastest butterfly in the garden. I think he likes to play games."

Mia grinned, watching Flash zoom between flowers. "I can see that! He looks like he's always in a hurry."

"And that's Sunny," Lucy added, pointing to the monarch resting on a milkweed leaf. "Sunny brings warmth and joy to every flower she visits. She's like the garden's little ray of sunshine."

Ben chuckled. "I like that! It's like each butterfly has its own personality."

Sophia looked thoughtful. "Do you think they remember us when they come back?"

Lucy nodded, smiling. "I think so. I like to imagine that they come back because they feel at home here."

The more Lucy watched the butterflies, the more she felt connected to each one. Her little visitors weren't just part of her garden; they were part of her imagination, filling her world with color, stories, and dreams.

One evening, as the sun was setting and the garden was bathed in a warm golden glow, Lucy sat quietly, watching her butterflies drift lazily among the flowers. She thought about all the stories she'd created for each one, and how they'd become more than just insects—they were her garden friends, her little characters who brought her world to life.

Her dad came over, noticing her deep in thought. "What are you thinking about, Lucy?" he asked, sitting down beside her.

She smiled, looking up at him. "I was just thinking about all the butterflies I've named. Each one has its own story. There's Sunny, who brings joy, and Flash, who's the fastest, and Sky, the explorer..."

Her dad nodded, a gentle smile on his face. "You've given them personalities, just like friends."

Lucy looked back at the garden, feeling a warm sense of happiness. "Yeah. It feels like they're my garden family."

Her dad put an arm around her shoulders. "That's because you've created a place that's full of love and care. The butterflies are drawn to it, and your imagination makes it even more magical."

As the sky turned shades of pink and orange, Lucy watched Sunny, Flash, and Sky as they floated through the garden, each one fitting perfectly into the world she had created. She realized that her garden wasn't just a collection of flowers and plants—it was a place filled with life, stories, and magic, where every visitor was welcome and loved.

With a heart full of joy, Lucy whispered to her butterflies, "Thank you for being here, my friends. You make my garden come alive." And as the last rays of sunlight faded, she knew that each butterfly, whether named or yet to be discovered, would always hold a special place in her garden and in her heart.

Chapter 13: Weather Woes

One evening, as Lucy sat by her window, she noticed dark clouds gathering on the horizon. The sky was painted in ominous shades of grey, and a gusty wind rustled through the trees. She felt a pang of worry as she thought about her garden, which was filled with delicate flowers and her butterfly friends.

As the wind picked up, Lucy ran outside to take one last look at her garden before the storm arrived. The zinnias and marigolds swayed in the strong breeze, their bright blooms looking vulnerable against the darkening sky. She bent down, whispering softly to each flower, hoping they would be okay.

"Please stay strong, little ones," she murmured, gently touching a milkweed leaf. She glanced around, half-expecting to see Sunny, Flash, or Sky flitting around, but they must have sensed the storm coming and were already tucked away, safe from the wind.

Lucy's mom joined her, a concerned look on her face. "It looks like a big storm is coming, Lucy. Let's go inside and wait it out."

Lucy's heart sank as she looked back at her garden, which had become her special place filled with life and color. "But what if the flowers get damaged?" she asked, her voice trembling a little. "Or what if the butterflies don't come back?"

Her mom placed a comforting arm around her. "Nature has a way of taking care of itself, Lucy. Flowers, plants, and animals face all kinds of challenges, but they're often stronger than they look. Let's see how your garden holds up—sometimes, things come back even stronger after a storm."

Lucy nodded, though she still felt a knot of worry in her stomach. She took one last look at her flowers before following her mom inside.

As the storm began, Lucy sat by the window, watching rain pour down in heavy sheets, turning the garden into a blur of colors. Lightning flashed across the sky, and thunder rumbled, shaking the walls of the house. The wind whipped through the yard, and Lucy could only imagine how her flowers must be bending under the force of the storm. She felt helpless, unable to do anything but watch and hope.

The storm raged on through the night, and Lucy went to bed with thoughts of her garden swirling in her mind. She worried that the flowers might be damaged or the soil washed away, undoing all the hard work she'd put in.

The next morning, Lucy woke up early and rushed outside, bracing herself for what she might find. As she reached her garden, her heart sank at the sight. Some flowers were bent, their stems drooping under the weight of rainwater. A few petals had scattered across the soil, and several of the smaller plants looked worse for wear.

She knelt down, touching a soggy marigold, sadness washing over her. "Oh, no... it looks like they got hurt," she whispered.

Just then, her dad joined her, watching as she gently touched the rain-soaked plants. "Storms can be tough on gardens," he said gently. "But give them some time. Plants are surprisingly resilient."

Lucy looked up at him, her expression doubtful. "You think they'll really be okay?"

He nodded. "Nature has a way of bouncing back. Let's help them out a bit. Why don't we gently shake off the water from the flowers and straighten any stems that got bent?"

Feeling a little more hopeful, Lucy began to carefully shake the rainwater from the blooms, watching as each flower lifted its head slightly. She straightened the stems, giving them a bit of support, and smoothed the soil around the roots to give them a stable foundation.

As she worked, she noticed something incredible: a few of the stronger plants were already standing tall, as if they had weathered the storm with determination. The milkweed, in particular, seemed unaffected, its leaves bright and full of life. She couldn't help but feel a spark of pride in seeing how tough her plants could be.

By the afternoon, with the sun shining down again, the garden began to dry out, and Lucy felt a sense of relief. She noticed that some of her butterfly friends had already returned, flitting around the flowers, seemingly unfazed by the previous night's storm. Flash, the bright yellow butterfly, was darting between blooms with his usual energy, while Sunny the monarch perched gracefully on a marigold, as if to reassure her that all was well.

Her friends Mia, Ben, and Sophia stopped by later in the day to see how the garden had fared.

"Oh no, did the storm hurt your flowers?" Ben asked, his face full of concern.

"A little bit," Lucy admitted. "But they're stronger than I thought. I think they'll bounce back." She smiled, feeling proud of her garden's resilience.

Mia nodded, gently touching a coneflower that had sprung back up. "It's amazing that they're still standing. Nature is so tough."

Sophia smiled at Lucy. "And it's because you took such good care of them that they could survive the storm. They're lucky to have you looking after them."

Lucy felt her heart swell with happiness as she looked over her garden, which was slowly coming back to life. She realized that her plants and flowers were tougher than she had ever imagined, able to face challenges and bounce back with strength and grace.

That evening, as she watched the sun set over her garden, Lucy felt a deep sense of pride—not just for her plants, but for the lessons they had taught her. She had learned that storms and challenges were a natural part of life, and that sometimes, the most beautiful things came from resilience and strength.

She whispered softly to her garden, "Thank you for being strong. I'm so proud of you."

As she turned to go inside, Lucy knew that the next time a storm came, she would worry less and trust more, knowing that her garden—and everything within it—was built to withstand life's challenges, and that with care and patience, beauty could bloom again.

Chapter 14: A Surprise from Grandpa

Lucy's garden had become a special place, a little world of colour, life, and resilience. But she never imagined it would bring her closer to someone very dear to her—her grandpa.

One sunny afternoon, as Lucy was busy watering her flowers, she heard the familiar sound of Grandpa's old truck rumbling down the driveway. She looked up, her face lighting up with excitement. Grandpa visited often, and he always brought interesting stories about plants and animals. He'd been a gardener for years, and Lucy loved hearing his tales of the gardens he had grown and all the plants he'd nurtured.

Grandpa stepped out of the truck, a warm smile on his face, and waved at her. "Hello, Lucy-girl! I brought you a little something for your garden."

Lucy hurried over, her curiosity piqued. Grandpa was holding a small pot with a tall, leafy plant that she hadn't seen before. It had clusters of purple flowers that looked delicate and inviting, each one shaped like a tiny trumpet.

"Grandpa! What is it?" Lucy asked, her eyes wide with wonder.

He knelt down beside her, setting the plant on the ground so she could get a closer look. "This, my dear, is a butterfly bush. Butterflies are drawn to it like bees to honey. It's one of the best plants you can have if you want to keep those beautiful creatures coming back to your garden."

Lucy's face lit up with excitement. "A butterfly bush! I've never seen one before. Thank you so much, Grandpa!" She threw her arms around him, hugging him tightly.

Grandpa chuckled, patting her back. "I knew you'd like it. I had one in my garden when I was younger, and I remember it being covered in butterflies. I thought this little bush might make your garden feel even more magical."

They walked together to her garden, and Grandpa found a sunny spot near the center to plant the butterfly bush. He showed Lucy how to carefully loosen the soil around the plant's roots and gently place it into the ground. Together, they patted the soil down, giving the bush a strong foundation.

As they worked, Grandpa shared stories of the gardens he had tended over the years. "I remember my first garden," he said, his eyes twinkling with fond memories. "I had rows of zinnias and sunflowers, and I'd watch butterflies and bees dance through them all day. There's something special about watching a garden come alive."

Lucy listened intently, her heart warmed by the thought of her grandpa tending to his own butterfly visitors when he was her age. She realized that her love for the garden came from him; it was like a connection that stretched through generations.

When they finished planting the butterfly bush, Lucy poured water around its roots, watching the soil absorb the moisture. "Do you think the butterflies will come soon?" she asked, glancing up at Grandpa.

He smiled, nodding. "They'll be here before you know it. Once those flowers bloom, you'll have butterflies visiting from near and far, all thanks to this little bush."

Lucy beamed with pride and excitement, imagining her garden filled with even more butterflies. "Thank you, Grandpa. This is the best surprise ever."

Over the next few days, Lucy tended to the butterfly bush with special care, making sure it had plenty of water and sunlight. She checked on it every morning, watching as the tiny buds started to open, revealing clusters of deep purple flowers. They had a faint, sweet scent, and she could already see how inviting they would be to her butterfly friends.

Then, one warm afternoon, as she was kneeling by the bush, she noticed her first visitor—a beautiful swallowtail butterfly with wings as black as midnight and bright yellow stripes. It fluttered down and landed on the butterfly bush, sipping nectar from one of the tiny flowers.

Lucy held her breath, watching the butterfly in awe. She named it Stripe, imagining it was the first of many to come. She felt a rush of gratitude toward her grandpa, who had given her such a special gift.

A few days later, Grandpa came over to see how the butterfly bush was doing. Lucy proudly showed him the blooms, which were now covered in butterflies of all colors. Monarchs, painted ladies, and swallowtails danced around the bush, drawn in by its sweet fragrance.

"See, Grandpa? They love it!" Lucy said, her face glowing with happiness.

Grandpa's eyes softened as he watched the butterflies flitting from bloom to bloom. "You did a beautiful job, Lucy. This garden of yours is truly something special. It's like watching a little piece of nature's magic."

Lucy looked up at him, feeling a deep sense of connection. "Thank you for helping me make it even better, Grandpa. Every time I see a butterfly on this bush, I'll think of you."

They sat together by the garden, quietly watching the butterflies. Lucy felt a warmth in her heart, a special bond with her grandpa that went beyond words. The butterfly bush wasn't just a plant—it was a gift that had deepened their connection and would remind her of him every time she saw a butterfly perched on its blooms.

As the sun began to set, Lucy looked around her garden, now more beautiful than she'd ever imagined. Each butterfly that visited felt like a little thank-you from the garden, a reminder of her grandpa's love and the magic they'd created together.

In that moment, Lucy knew her butterfly garden was more than a dream—it was a place where memories, love, and life would always bloom. And whenever she saw a butterfly land on the purple flowers, she'd smile, knowing that her grandpa's gift had become a special part of her garden's story.

Chapter 15: The Butterfly's Life Cycle

It was a warm morning, and Lucy was tending to her garden, carefully watering each plant when something tiny and green caught her eye. There, on a milkweed leaf, was a small caterpillar, munching away happily. Lucy's heart skipped a beat—she'd read about caterpillars and butterflies, but she'd never seen the beginning of the butterfly life cycle in her own garden before.

She knelt down, her eyes wide with wonder as she watched the caterpillar munch its way across the leaf. It had black, white, and yellow stripes, and it moved slowly, chewing in tiny bites. She realized this was her chance to witness the entire transformation from caterpillar to butterfly, right here in her own garden. The thought filled her with excitement.

"Mom! Dad!" Lucy called, still kneeling by the milkweed plant.

Her parents came over, smiling as they saw her pointing at the caterpillar. "Look!" Lucy said. "A caterpillar! Do you think it's going to become a butterfly?"

Her dad smiled, nodding. "It just might, Lucy. You're lucky—it looks like it's a monarch caterpillar, and monarchs love milkweed. You've created the perfect spot for it."

Lucy's mom leaned in, studying the caterpillar. "You're getting the chance to see the whole life cycle of a butterfly, Lucy. It's a rare and beautiful thing to watch. Caterpillars need to eat a lot before they're ready for the next stage, so keep an eye on it. It's going to change right before your eyes."

Lucy couldn't believe it. She was about to witness the transformation she'd only read about. She gently touched the milkweed leaf next to the caterpillar, careful not to disturb it. Her heart filled with excitement as she imagined watching it grow, knowing that one day it would become a butterfly, just like the ones that visited her garden every day.

Over the next few days, Lucy visited the caterpillar every morning and afternoon. She watched as it munched on leaf after leaf, its tiny body growing plumper and longer with each passing day. She was amazed by how much it ate, but she remembered from her books that caterpillars needed lots of food to build up energy for the next phase of their life cycle.

Lucy began recording her observations in her notebook. She drew little sketches of the caterpillar each day, noting how it was growing bigger and stronger. She learned that this stage was called the "larva" stage, where caterpillars focused on eating and growing as much as possible.

One afternoon, Lucy noticed something she hadn't seen before. As the caterpillar nibbled on a leaf, she saw a tiny white dot on a nearby leaf—a butterfly egg! It was no bigger than a pinhead, and she realized that this must be where the caterpillar's journey had started. Her books had mentioned that butterflies lay eggs on host plants like milkweed, where the caterpillars would have plenty of food once they hatched.

"Mom, look!" she called, pointing to the egg.

Her mom knelt down, smiling as she saw the tiny egg. "That's where every butterfly's journey begins. First an egg, then a caterpillar, and then they move on to the next stages. It's an incredible journey."

Lucy felt a sense of awe as she looked at the egg and then back at the caterpillar, realizing just how much it had grown from a tiny dot like that. She imagined the journey it had already been on and the amazing transformation it still had ahead.

After several days of watching the caterpillar grow and eat, Lucy noticed a change. One morning, instead of munching on leaves, the caterpillar had crawled to the underside of a branch and was hanging there in a "J" shape. She gasped, recognizing the signal from her books—this was the beginning of the chrysalis stage.

"Oh, it's happening!" she whispered, barely able to contain her excitement.

Lucy checked on the caterpillar constantly, marveling at the sight. By afternoon, it had shed its outer skin and transformed into a smooth, green chrysalis. It hung from the branch, shimmering in the sunlight, with a delicate gold line near the top, almost like a crown. It was more beautiful than Lucy had imagined.

Her mom joined her in the garden, admiring the chrysalis. "Now comes the real magic, Lucy. Inside that chrysalis, the caterpillar will transform completely, turning into a butterfly. It's called metamorphosis."

Lucy nodded, her eyes fixed on the chrysalis. "It's like a secret happening right here in my garden," she said softly. "I can't wait to see what it looks like when it's ready."

Her dad came over, smiling as he heard her. "It'll take a couple of weeks, so you'll need a bit of patience. But when it finally emerges, it'll be worth every moment of waiting."

Every day, Lucy checked on the chrysalis, watching for any signs of change. She spent her mornings sketching it in her notebook, noting how its color stayed a deep green. She felt a mix of excitement and anticipation, imagining the day when the chrysalis would begin to darken, signalling that a butterfly was ready to emerge.

Then, one morning, as she was watering her garden, she noticed something different about the chrysalis. It had turned darker, and she could just make out faint colors within—orange and black, the same colors as a monarch's wings. Lucy's heart raced. The transformation was almost complete.

For the rest of the day, Lucy kept an eye on the chrysalis, barely able to contain her excitement. And then, just before sunset, she saw a tiny crack appear. She held her breath as the crack grew larger, and soon, the chrysalis split open, and a damp, fragile butterfly began to emerge. Its wings were crumpled at first, but it slowly stretched them out, letting them dry and harden in the evening air.

Lucy's heart filled with joy as she watched the butterfly's wings grow stronger, the orange and black patterns glistening in the sunlight. This was it—the caterpillar's final transformation, from a tiny egg to a beautiful butterfly.

Her parents joined her, both of them smiling proudly as they watched the butterfly flex its wings, preparing for its first flight.

"You did it," her mom whispered to Lucy. "You witnessed the whole journey, from the very beginning."

Lucy felt a deep sense of wonder as the butterfly finally took off, fluttering around her garden, visiting the flowers that had nourished it from its caterpillar days. She realized that she had just witnessed a miracle, a transformation that had unfolded right before her eyes. The garden she had worked so hard to create had become the perfect home for a life cycle that was as beautiful as it was magical.

From that day forward, every time Lucy saw a butterfly in her garden, she remembered the caterpillar, the chrysalis, and the incredible journey it had taken. And as she looked around at her garden, filled with flowers, butterflies, and memories, she knew that each visitor was a reminder of nature's amazing power to transform, grow, and create beauty in the world.

Chapter 16: A Special Caterpillar

A few weeks after witnessing the transformation of her first caterpillar, Lucy's garden was buzzing with life again. Butterflies flitted from flower to flower, bees hummed happily, and Mr. Hummingbird made his daily visits to the butterfly bush. But one morning, as Lucy inspected her milkweed plants, she spotted another tiny caterpillar munching away on a leaf.

She knelt down, smiling as she watched it nibble. This caterpillar was small and wiggly, with black, white, and yellow stripes—just like the one she'd seen before. But something about this one felt special, and she decided then and there to name him "Curly" after his tiny, curled body.

"Hello, Curly," Lucy whispered with a gentle smile. "I can't wait to watch you grow and see you become a butterfly, just like the others."

Lucy felt a surge of excitement at the thought of watching Curly's transformation journey. She remembered every detail of the last caterpillar's life cycle and was thrilled to witness it all over again. Curly was like her little garden companion, and she couldn't wait to see him grow stronger each day.

Over the next few days, Lucy visited Curly each morning, eager to check on his progress. She watched as he devoured leaf after leaf, his tiny body growing plumper and longer. Curly was quite the eater, and Lucy couldn't help but laugh as she watched him nibble his way through the milkweed leaves, leaving little trails of holes in his wake.

Lucy documented everything in her notebook, writing down Curly's growth and sketching his appearance each day. She loved noting all the little details, from his tiny feet gripping the leaf to the way he curled up to rest after a big meal.

Her friends Mia, Ben, and Sophia came over one afternoon to see Curly.

"Look at him go!" Ben said, laughing as he watched Curly munch away. "He's got quite the appetite!"

Lucy grinned. "He sure does! I think he's getting ready for the next stage. Soon, he'll turn into a chrysalis, just like the first caterpillar."

Sophia knelt down beside Lucy, watching Curly with wide eyes. "It's amazing to think that one day, he'll be a butterfly."

Mia nodded. "It's like he's getting ready for something magical. I can't wait to see him become a butterfly, too!"

Lucy felt a warm sense of pride as her friends shared her excitement. Curly wasn't just a caterpillar; he was a part of her garden family, and his transformation felt like a shared experience with everyone who had helped her garden grow.

One morning, after days of watching Curly eat and grow, Lucy noticed something different. Curly had stopped munching and was crawling to the underside of a sturdy branch on the milkweed. Lucy recognized the behaviour immediately—Curly was getting ready to form his chrysalis.

Her heart raced with excitement as she watched him attach himself to the branch with a silk thread, curling into the familiar "J" shape that signalled the next stage. She couldn't wait to see him enter the chrysalis stage, knowing that this was the beginning of an incredible transformation.

"Mom! Dad! Curly's starting his chrysalis!" she called, her voice brimming with joy.

Her parents joined her, watching as Curly shed his outer skin and revealed a beautiful green chrysalis underneath. The chrysalis was smooth and shiny, with a golden band around the top, just like the last one she had seen. Lucy marvelled at its delicate beauty, feeling a deep sense of wonder.

"It's amazing every time, isn't it?" her dad said, smiling at her.

Lucy nodded, her eyes fixed on Curly's chrysalis. "It really is. I feel like I'm watching something magical happen right here in my garden."

As the days went by, Lucy checked on Curly's chrysalis each morning. She noted any changes she saw, and her anticipation grew with each passing day. She couldn't help but imagine the moment Curly would finally emerge, a fully transformed butterfly, ready to take flight.

One afternoon, Mia, Ben, and Sophia returned to check on Curly. Lucy showed them the chrysalis, explaining that it would soon darken, signalling that Curly was almost ready to emerge.

"Isn't it amazing?" Lucy said, beaming. "He's been in there for over a week, and soon he'll be a butterfly."

Ben grinned. "Curly's about to have his big moment!"

Finally, after days of waiting, Lucy noticed the chrysalis turning darker. She could just make out the faint outline of wings within, the orange and black patterns becoming visible through the delicate casing. Her heart filled with excitement—Curly was almost ready to make his debut.

The next morning, Lucy rushed outside and gasped. The chrysalis was splitting open, and a small, fragile butterfly was emerging. Curly's wings were crumpled at first, but he clung to the branch, gently stretching them out as they dried in the sun. The orange and black patterns of a monarch butterfly slowly appeared, just as vibrant and beautiful as Lucy had imagined.

"Mom! Dad! He's here! Curly's a butterfly!" Lucy shouted, her voice filled with pride.

Her parents hurried over, both of them smiling as they watched Curly spread his wings, taking in his new world for the first time.

Lucy's friends arrived just in time to see Curly make his first flight. They gathered around, their eyes wide with awe as Curly lifted off from the branch, fluttering his new wings in the morning sunlight.

"He's beautiful," Sophia whispered, her voice full of wonder.

Lucy felt a deep sense of joy and accomplishment as she watched Curly soar into the garden, joining the other butterflies flitting from flower to flower. She realized that witnessing Curly's journey from caterpillar to butterfly had taught her so much—not only about nature's miracles but about patience, resilience, and the beauty of transformation.

As Curly disappeared into the garden, Lucy knew that her butterfly friends were more than just visitors—they were part of the magic that made her garden come alive. And with each butterfly that fluttered by, she felt grateful for the chance to be part of their journey, watching the cycle of life unfold right before her eyes.

Chapter 17: Lucy's Science Project

Lucy's garden had become a place of endless wonder, and she couldn't stop thinking about everything she'd learned about butterflies and their life cycle. One afternoon, as she was watching butterflies dance around her flowers, she had an idea—a science project! She could share her experiences with her classmates, teaching them about butterflies, the life cycle, and all the amazing things she'd witnessed in her garden.

The next day at school, Lucy talked to her teacher, Ms. Martinez, about her idea. "I've been growing a butterfly garden at home, and I thought I could make it into a science project!" she said, her eyes sparkling with excitement.

Ms. Martinez smiled, clearly intrigued. "That sounds like a wonderful idea, Lucy! Sharing what you've observed about butterflies would make a fantastic project. You can cover the life cycle, their favourite plants, and maybe even share some of the sketches and notes you've been keeping."

Lucy beamed. She felt excited to start working on it and to finally share everything she had learned with her friends and classmates. She spent the rest of the day brainstorming ideas and couldn't wait to get started on her project board.

That weekend, Lucy set up a space in her room to work on her project. She gathered her notebook, her sketches, and all the notes she'd made about Curly and the other butterflies she'd named. She decided her project would cover the four main stages of a butterfly's life cycle: egg, caterpillar, chrysalis, and adult butterfly. She would include pictures, drawings, and even some facts she'd learned from her library books.

With her mom's help, Lucy created a colorful title for her board: "The Life Cycle of a Butterfly." She chose bright orange and yellow letters to mimic the colors of a monarch butterfly, and she decorated the corners with little paper butterflies she cut out herself.

For each stage, Lucy created a special section on the board:

The Egg Stage

She included a photo of the tiny white dot she had seen on the milkweed leaf and wrote, "This is where every butterfly's life begins. A butterfly lays its eggs on host plants like milkweed so the caterpillars will have food right when they hatch."

The Caterpillar Stage

Lucy added a few of her sketches of Curly and other caterpillars she'd observed, showing how they grew bigger each day by munching on milkweed leaves. She explained, "Caterpillars eat a lot to gather energy for their transformation. They can grow several times their original size!"

The Chrysalis Stage

For this section, Lucy used a photo of Curly's chrysalis and wrote about how the caterpillar forms a protective casing around itself. She explained, "Inside the chrysalis, the caterpillar completely transforms. This process is called metamorphosis."

The Butterfly Stage

Lucy included a beautiful drawing she made of Curly as a fully grown monarch butterfly. She wrote, "After about two weeks, the butterfly emerges from the chrysalis, ready to take flight and explore. Butterflies help pollinate flowers and add color to the garden."

Lucy was thrilled with how the project was coming together. She added a section at the bottom of the board titled "Did You Know?" Here, she included fun facts about butterflies: that they taste with their feet, that they can see colors we can't, and that they're important pollinators, just like bees.

Finally, Lucy added one more personal touch—a small photo of her butterfly garden, surrounded by flowers and buzzing with life. She wrote a short note beneath it: "My butterfly garden has taught me so much about nature's magic. Watching butterflies transform has been like watching a miracle happen in my backyard."

When she finished, Lucy stood back to admire her work. She felt a deep sense of pride, knowing that her project was not only about butterflies but about everything she'd experienced and learned in her garden.

The day of the science fair finally arrived, and Lucy set up her project in the classroom. Her classmates wandered over to see her board, and their faces lit up with curiosity as they read through each stage of the life cycle.

Her friend Ben was especially impressed. "Lucy, this is amazing! I didn't know caterpillars ate so much before they turned into butterflies."

Mia chimed in, pointing at the chrysalis photo. "And I didn't know they transformed inside a chrysalis. It's like they're hiding a secret until they're ready!"

Lucy smiled, happy that her classmates were learning something new. She explained how she'd watched Curly and other caterpillars in her garden, sharing the excitement of seeing them grow, change, and take flight.

When Ms. Martinez visited her project, she nodded approvingly. "Lucy, you've put together such a thoughtful project. You've gone beyond just learning facts—you've experienced the whole process firsthand. Your passion for butterflies shines through."

Lucy felt her cheeks warm with pride. "Thank you, Ms. Martinez. I've loved learning about butterflies, and I wanted to share that with everyone."

As the science fair went on, Lucy realized that her project had given her more than just knowledge about butterflies—it had given her a chance to connect with her classmates, sharing the magic of transformation and nature's resilience. She felt grateful for her garden, her butterfly friends, and the special experiences she'd had that had made this project possible.

At the end of the day, as she carefully packed up her project, Lucy felt a deep sense of accomplishment. She'd shared her garden's story with her friends, opening a little window into the world of butterflies, transformation, and growth.

And as she headed home, Lucy knew her love for butterflies would keep growing, her garden continuing to be a place of learning, wonder, and beauty for as long as butterflies called it home.

Chapter 18: The Garden Grows

Lucy's garden had flourished beyond her wildest dreams. Everywhere she looked, flowers were blooming—zinnias, marigolds, coneflowers, and the butterfly bush her grandpa had given her, each adding its own splash of color and fragrance. Butterflies visited daily, gliding through the air and landing gracefully on the bright petals. Mr. Hummingbird still made his regular stops, sipping from his favourite flowers, while bees hummed around, busy as ever.

As the days passed, more butterflies seemed to find their way to her little paradise. Neighbours walking by began to pause, admiring the colorful scene. Children pointed excitedly at the butterflies, and even adults would stop to take in the beauty of Lucy's thriving garden.

One afternoon, as Lucy was tending to her plants, her neighbour Mrs. Collins stopped by. She leaned over the fence, smiling warmly. "Lucy, your garden is just marvellous! I haven't seen so many butterflies in one place in a long time. You've created something truly special."

Lucy beamed with pride. "Thank you, Mrs. Collins! It started as a small project, but I love watching it grow."

As more neighbours visited, admiring her flowers and the many butterflies, Lucy began to feel a spark of inspiration. She realized that her garden had become a magical place, one she wanted to share with everyone. But how could she share it in a meaningful way?

One evening, as she watered her garden and thought about how it had grown, an idea came to her—she could have an open garden day! She could invite her neighbours, friends, and even her classmates to experience the wonder of butterflies, just as she did each day. Her garden could be a place for everyone to enjoy, learn, and connect with nature.

Lucy's heart raced with excitement as she imagined what the open day might look like. She pictured colorful signs guiding guests through different sections of the garden, little tags identifying each type of flower, and a "Butterfly Observation Spot" where visitors could sit quietly and watch the butterflies up close.

As soon as she went inside, Lucy grabbed her notebook and began jotting down her ideas:

Welcome Sign: A bright, cheerful sign welcoming everyone to the garden.

Flower Tags: Small tags by each plant, with names like "Zinnia," "Marigold," and "Butterfly Bush" so people could learn about each flower.

Butterfly Observation Spot: A cozy spot with benches or small seats where guests could sit and watch butterflies in peace.

Garden Tour: A simple path that guided guests through the flowers, showing them the best spots to see butterflies and bees.

Information Table: A small table with fun facts about butterflies, pollinators, and the life cycle she'd shared in her science project.

Lucy felt a thrill of excitement as she thought about how much fun it would be to share her knowledge, helping others see the magic of her butterfly garden. But as she looked at her list, she realized there was still some work to do before she was ready to open the garden to everyone.

"Maybe not just yet," she murmured to herself. "I want everything to be perfect."

She decided to take her time, adding a few special touches to the garden and learning as much as she could so she'd be ready to answer questions. She also wanted to make sure the butterflies felt safe and at home, even with more visitors around.

Over the following weeks, Lucy kept working on her garden, planning for the open day while still enjoying the peace of her little sanctuary. She added a few more plants she'd learned butterflies loved, like asters and verbena, to make the garden even more inviting. She created small, handwritten labels for each flower, placing them in front of each plant so she could get used to having them ready for guests.

Every now and then, her friends Mia, Ben, and Sophia would stop by, and Lucy would show them the new additions and share her plans.

"Are you really going to invite the whole neighbourhood?" Ben asked one afternoon, his eyes wide with excitement.

Lucy nodded, her face glowing. "Yes! I want everyone to see the butterflies and feel the magic of the garden. But I want to wait until it's just right."

Mia grinned. "You're going to be like a garden tour guide! I bet everyone will love it."

Sophia added, "And you could even share some of the stories you've made up about the butterflies! It's like they're the stars of your garden."

Lucy laughed, already imagining Sunny, Flash, and the other butterflies as the "official greeters" on her garden tour. "I'll definitely share their stories," she agreed. "I want everyone to see them as part of the garden family."

As Lucy continued preparing, word about her garden spread through the neighbourhood. Soon, people would wave at her as they walked by, commenting on how beautiful her garden looked and how much they loved seeing the butterflies. Lucy felt her heart swell with pride each time, knowing she'd created a place of beauty that was brightening people's days.

One evening, as she sat outside with her mom and dad, enjoying the sight of butterflies fluttering around the flowers, she shared her plans with them.

"I'm going to have an open day," she announced, a mix of excitement and nerves in her voice. "But not yet—I want it to be perfect first. I'll give everyone a tour and show them the butterflies up close. Maybe I can even teach them a little about the life cycle."

Her mom smiled, reaching over to squeeze her hand. "I think that's a wonderful idea, Lucy. You've put so much love into this garden, and sharing it with others is a beautiful way to spread that joy."

Her dad nodded in agreement. "And I'm sure everyone will learn a lot from you. You've become quite the butterfly expert."

Lucy felt a surge of confidence. She knew the open day would take time and a bit more preparation, but she was determined to make it as special as possible. She wanted her neighbours and friends to feel the same sense of wonder and connection that she felt every time she walked through her garden.

As the sun set, painting the sky in shades of pink and orange, Lucy looked around at her garden, feeling grateful for every flower, every butterfly, and every moment she'd spent caring for them. Her dream was no longer just her own—it was a place she could share with her community, a little patch of magic that belonged to everyone who visited.

And as the last rays of sunlight faded, Lucy knew that her garden's story was still growing, just like the flowers and the butterflies. When the time was right, she'd open it to the world, inviting everyone to experience the beauty, peace, and wonder of her very own butterfly haven.

Chapter 19: Sharing the Joy

The day Lucy had been waiting for had finally arrived. After weeks of planning and preparing, she was ready to host a small "garden tour" for her friends and family. She'd worked tirelessly to get everything just right—adding flower tags, setting up a cozy observation spot, and arranging a small table with butterfly facts and a few of her favourite garden sketches.

As the afternoon sun cast a warm glow over her garden, Lucy put the finishing touches on her welcome sign, which read, "Welcome to Lucy's Butterfly Haven!" Brightly coloured paper butterflies fluttered on either side of the sign, adding a touch of whimsy.

Her mom and dad helped set up chairs along the garden path, and her friends Mia, Ben, and Sophia arrived early to help as well. They couldn't hide their excitement as they looked around, admiring how beautifully everything had come together.

"This is amazing, Lucy!" Mia said, grinning. "It's like a real garden tour."

Ben nodded, looking at the flower tags with interest. "And you even put names on the plants! I love it."

Lucy beamed with pride, feeling grateful for the help and support of her friends. "Thanks, everyone! I wanted it to feel special for you and everyone else. I can't wait to show you around."

As her family and a few close neighbours arrived, Lucy felt a mix of excitement and nerves. But as soon as she began the tour, all her nervousness melted away. She felt like she was sharing a secret, a little piece of magic, with the people she cared about.

Starting at the entrance, Lucy led the group down the winding path through the flowers, stopping by each plant to share fun facts. She introduced her guests to each section of the garden, explaining why she had chosen certain flowers and how each one helped attract butterflies.

At each stop, she sprinkled in her favourite facts, like how butterflies taste with their feet and how they're drawn to bright colors.

She could see the curiosity and delight in everyone's faces, especially when she took them to the "Butterfly Observation Spot." It was a cozy corner with a few small seats and a clear view of the butterfly bush and milkweed, where butterflies were already resting.

"Here's where you can sit quietly and just watch," Lucy explained. "If you stay still, the butterflies will come close enough to see every little detail on their wings."

As her friends and family settled down in the observation spot, they were greeted by familiar faces: Sunny the monarch, Flash the yellow butterfly, and even Mr. Hummingbird, who zipped by, creating a chorus of "oohs" and "ahhs."

Lucy grinned, thrilled that her butterfly friends were making an appearance. It felt like they, too, were part of her garden family, welcoming the visitors with open wings.

"Do you all want to hear a story about the butterflies?" Lucy asked, looking around at the eager faces.

Everyone nodded, so she told them about Sunny, Flash, and Sky, sharing the personalities she had imagined for each butterfly. Her audience listened intently, laughing and smiling as she recounted the adventures of her butterfly friends. Her dad gave her an encouraging nod, clearly proud of her storytelling.

When they reached the table with butterfly facts and sketches, Lucy invited everyone to look through her notebook, where she'd drawn each stage of the butterfly's life cycle and kept notes about her observations. She showed them sketches of Curly, the caterpillar who had transformed right before her eyes.

Her grandpa looked at her sketches, his eyes crinkling with pride. "Lucy, these are wonderful! You've learned so much and created something beautiful."

Lucy's heart swelled with happiness. She loved sharing her knowledge and seeing how her garden had brought so much joy to others. As the tour continued, she answered questions about the butterflies and their habits, her excitement growing with each new conversation.

Finally, as the tour wrapped up, Lucy gathered everyone in the observation spot for a thank-you.

"I just want to say thank you to all of you," she began, her voice warm and heartfelt. "This garden started as my dream, but you all helped make it special. It's our place now—a little piece of nature for all of us."

Her friends and family clapped, some even wiping away happy tears. Lucy's mom hugged her tightly. "You've given us a beautiful gift, Lucy. Thank you for sharing it with us."

As everyone lingered in the garden, talking, laughing, and watching the butterflies, Lucy felt an overwhelming sense of joy and accomplishment. Her garden had become a haven not just for butterflies, but for her family, her friends, and even her neighbours.

When the sun began to set, painting the sky in soft shades of pink and orange, Lucy sat down on one of the garden seats, feeling a quiet peace settle over her. Her garden tour had been everything she'd hoped for—filled with beauty, laughter, and a shared love for nature.

As she watched her friends and family make their way home, she whispered a thank-you to the butterflies and the flowers that had made her garden such a special place. Lucy knew this was just the beginning of many more days spent sharing the joy of her butterfly haven, a place where life, love, and nature bloomed together.

Chapter 20: The Monarch Migration

The crisp days of autumn were beginning to settle in, and Lucy noticed subtle changes in her garden. The flowers were still blooming brightly, and the butterflies still visited each day, but there was something different in the air. Her monarch butterflies, especially Sunny and a few others, seemed more active, fluttering from flower to flower with an extra sense of purpose.

One afternoon, while browsing a book about butterflies from the library, Lucy stumbled upon a fascinating chapter: The Monarch Migration. Her eyes widened as she read about the extraordinary journey monarch butterflies made each year, traveling thousands of miles south to warmer climates before winter arrived.

"They migrate all the way to Mexico," Lucy whispered to herself, reading in awe. "It's a journey that can be over 2,500 miles long! They fly from places like Canada and the northern United States all the way south."

The thought of her monarch butterflies—perhaps even Sunny—making such an epic journey filled her with a mixture of wonder and longing. She imagined them flying in colorful clusters, the sky dotted with orange and black wings as they journeyed toward a new, warmer home.

Lucy eagerly shared her discovery with her parents over dinner that night. "Did you know monarch butterflies migrate thousands of miles to escape the cold? They go all the way to Mexico! And it takes them weeks, sometimes months, to get there."

Her dad looked impressed. "That's incredible! Butterflies seem so small and delicate, but they're clearly much stronger than they look."

Her mom nodded. "It sounds like monarchs are born adventurers, Lucy. And think about it—if they travel such a long way, they must see amazing things along the way."

Lucy thought about the journey monarchs must make and felt a thrill run through her. She wondered what sights they might encounter along the way—mountains, forests, rivers, and fields. She imagined Sunny, with her bright orange wings, flying with other monarchs, gliding over landscapes she'd never see herself. It was almost like a fairytale, but it was real, and it was happening every year.

That evening, Lucy decided to learn as much as she could about the monarch migration. She read that monarchs gather in large groups, sometimes numbering in the thousands, forming vibrant clouds of orange and black. They would rest on trees and plants along the way, covering branches so thickly it looked as if the trees themselves had turned orange. Lucy could hardly believe the images she found online and in her books—the sight of so many butterflies clustered together seemed like something out of a dream.

Her curiosity grew, and Lucy started noting down facts about the migration in her notebook:

Distance: Monarchs can travel up to 2,500 miles during their migration.

Wintering Grounds: They gather in forests in central Mexico, where the trees provide shelter and warmth.

Generations: It takes multiple generations of monarchs to complete the full migration cycle. The butterflies that reach Mexico will often be the great-grandchildren of those who left in spring.

Navigation: Monarchs are thought to navigate by sensing the position of the sun, though scientists are still learning how they find their way so accurately.

As she read, Lucy's imagination filled with visions of her garden butterflies setting off on this grand journey, traveling together in a flurry of wings, catching warm air currents, and resting under starlit skies. She hoped that someday, she might be able to see a monarch migration up close, to watch the butterflies she loved make their way south in one of nature's most awe-inspiring displays.

One weekend, Lucy shared her new fascination with her friends, Mia, Ben, and Sophia. She showed them the notes and pictures she had collected, and their eyes lit up with the same excitement she felt.

"Imagine Sunny going all the way to Mexico!" Mia said, her voice full of wonder. "That's so far."

Sophia looked thoughtful. "It's like they have their own secret path in the sky."

Ben nodded. "And they're so small, but they can fly all that way. It's like they're superhero butterflies!"

Inspired by her friends' enthusiasm, Lucy decided to make a small tribute to the monarch migration in her garden. She painted a little sign that read, "Safe Travels, Monarch Friends!" and placed it near the butterfly bush. She wanted her butterfly visitors to know they were loved and that she wished them a safe journey, even if they couldn't understand her words.

In the following days, Lucy spent extra time in the garden, watching the monarchs closely. She knew that soon they would be leaving, embarking on their long journey south. Part of her felt a little sad, knowing her butterflies would be gone for the winter, but she also felt a sense of pride, knowing they were off to join one of nature's greatest adventures.

One sunny afternoon, as Lucy sat in her observation spot, she watched Sunny land on the butterfly bush. She whispered softly, "I hope you have a safe journey, Sunny. I'll be here waiting for you next spring."

The butterfly lingered for a moment, its wings opening and closing gently, as if to say goodbye. Then, with a delicate lift of its wings, Sunny took off, fluttering gracefully into the air.

Lucy watched her disappear, a bittersweet feeling settling over her. She knew that by springtime, new generations of monarchs would return, maybe even some of Sunny's descendants. Her garden would once again be filled with butterflies, flowers, and life.

That night, as she drifted off to sleep, Lucy dreamed of butterflies flying in unison over mountains, forests, and fields, the moonlight guiding their path as they travelled south. She felt a connection to them, knowing that her garden had given them a place to grow, rest, and gather strength for their journey.

And as she slept, she felt a deep sense of peace, knowing that her little butterfly haven was part of something much larger—a beautiful cycle of life, adventure, and resilience that stretched beyond the borders of her garden and into the vast, wondrous world.

Chapter 21: Butterfly Friends Depart

Lucy began noticing changes in her garden. The flowers were still vibrant, but fewer butterflies visited each day. The lively buzz of summer was fading, replaced by a soft, gentle quietness that settled over her garden like a cozy blanket. While Lucy loved the warmth of autumn, she knew that the season brought with it a bittersweet farewell.

One afternoon, as she sat in her observation spot, Lucy noticed her familiar butterfly friends—Sunny, Flash, and Sky—moving with a new sense of urgency. They flitted from flower to flower, lingering on each bloom, as if savouring the last sips of nectar. She knew they were preparing for their journey south, a journey she had read so much about and one that filled her with both excitement and sadness.

"They're getting ready to leave, aren't they?" Lucy asked her mom, who had joined her in the garden.

Her mom smiled softly and nodded. "Yes, they are. Butterflies follow the seasons, and as the weather cools, they begin their migration. It's time for them to move on, but they'll return when the world warms up again."

Lucy nodded, feeling a mixture of pride and melancholy. She knew her butterflies were setting off on an incredible journey, one that would take them far from her little garden. But she couldn't help feeling sad, knowing that her garden would soon be quieter without their graceful presence.

In the following days, Lucy watched each butterfly with a careful eye, cherishing their visits as if they were special little goodbyes. She spent extra time by the butterfly bush and milkweed, hoping to catch a final glimpse of her butterfly friends before they left. Every time one of them fluttered away, she whispered a soft farewell, wishing them safe travels.

One morning, she found Flash, the bright yellow butterfly, resting on a marigold. She knelt down beside him, feeling a wave of gratitude. "Goodbye, Flash," she whispered, her voice tender. "You've brought so much joy to my garden. I hope you have a wonderful journey."

Flash lifted his wings, almost as if he were nodding in response, before taking off into the sky, his yellow wings catching the sunlight one last time. Lucy watched him until he disappeared from view, her heart aching with a quiet sadness, but also swelling with pride. She knew he was off to explore the world beyond her garden.

The next day, she noticed Sunny hovering near the butterfly bush, sipping nectar as usual. Lucy knelt down beside her, feeling a deep connection to this beautiful monarch butterfly who had been with her since the early days of summer. "Goodbye, Sunny," she whispered softly. "Thank you for making my garden so special. I'll see you again next spring."

Sunny lingered for a moment, her orange and black wings gently opening and closing. Then, with a final, graceful flutter, she rose into the sky, joining the other monarchs as they began their long journey south. Lucy watched her go, a tear slipping down her cheek, but she smiled through it, knowing Sunny was off to join the great monarch migration she had read so much about.

As more butterflies departed, Lucy felt a calm settle over her garden. She knew that even though her butterfly friends were leaving, they were fulfilling the natural cycle that had been happening for generations. Her garden had been a place of rest, food, and beauty for them, a home where they could gather strength before embarking on their journey.

Lucy decided to create a little tribute for her butterfly friends. She found some smooth stones and painted them with bright colors—orange and black for monarchs, yellow for Flash, and shades of blue for Sky. She arranged them around her butterfly bush, creating a small "Butterfly Farewell Garden" to honour the butterflies who had filled her summer with magic.

Her friends Mia, Ben, and Sophia came by to see the garden one afternoon, noticing the colorful stones.

"It's beautiful, Lucy," Mia said, her voice warm with admiration. "They'll always have a place here."

Lucy nodded, her heart full. "I wanted to make something that would remind me of them, even after they're gone. It's like they'll always be part of my garden."

Ben smiled, pointing to the stones. "It's like they're still here, in a way. And they'll come back in the spring, right?"

Lucy nodded, feeling a spark of hope. "Yes. Monarchs return every year, so some of them will be back. And they'll bring new butterflies with them."

As the weeks passed and the last butterflies left, Lucy's garden grew quieter, settling into the golden hues of autumn. She missed seeing her butterfly friends every day, but she felt a sense of pride knowing she had helped them prepare for their journey. Her garden had been a place of safety and beauty for them, and she knew they would carry a piece of it with them wherever they went.

One evening, as she watched the sun set over her garden, Lucy whispered a final farewell to her butterfly friends, knowing she'd see their descendants next spring. She felt a deep sense of peace, knowing that her garden was part of a much larger journey, one that stretched beyond her backyard and into the vast world.

And as she turned to go inside, Lucy felt a renewed sense of purpose. Next spring, she would be ready to welcome the butterflies back, creating an even more vibrant, welcoming garden for them to return to. She looked forward to watching new life bloom, knowing that each butterfly carried a piece of her garden's love and care with them, wherever they went.

Chapter 22: Autumn Changes

As autumn settled in, Lucy noticed new changes in her garden. The bright greens of summer were transforming into golden yellows, deep oranges, and warm reds. The air felt crisp, and the once-busy hum of butterflies, bees, and hummingbirds had quieted. Her garden was slowing down, preparing for the cooler weather.

One afternoon, as Lucy watered her flowers, her mom came outside, carrying a gardening book. "Are you ready to help your garden get ready for autumn, Lucy?" she asked, smiling.

Lucy looked around, realizing that her garden would need extra care to make it through the colder months. "Yes! I want to make sure everything stays healthy so it can come back strong next spring."

Together, they sat on the garden bench, flipping through pages filled with tips for autumn gardening. Lucy learned that autumn was a time for letting certain plants rest and for giving the soil the nutrients it needed to thrive in the next growing season. She felt excited to prepare her garden for this change, knowing it was just another part of the cycle.

"Some plants, like the annuals, won't survive the frost," her mom explained, pointing to the zinnias and marigolds. "But we can save seeds from them to plant next year."

Lucy's eyes lit up. "We can? So even if these plants won't come back, new ones can grow from the seeds?"

Her mom nodded, handing her a small pouch. "Exactly. We can gather seeds from the flowers now, and you can plant them again in the spring. It's like they're leaving a little gift for you."

Next, Lucy and her mom turned their attention to the butterfly bush and the milkweed. "Perennials, like the butterfly bush, will survive the winter," her mom explained. "But we need to trim them back and cover the roots to keep them warm."

Lucy watched as her mom showed her how to gently prune the butterfly bush, removing the old blooms and thinning the branches. She carefully trimmed the milkweed, which had been a favourite spot for her butterfly friends, and together, they spread a layer of mulch around the plants to keep them insulated from the frost.

As they worked, Lucy thought about how different her garden would look in winter. It wouldn't be as colorful or as full of life, but she felt comforted knowing that everything was resting, waiting to grow again. It reminded her of the butterflies, who had left for warmer places but would return when the world warmed up.

To help the soil stay rich and healthy, Lucy and her mom decided to add compost. They gently dug it into the garden beds, enriching the soil with nutrients. "This will help the plants grow strong next year," her mom said, smiling as they worked together. "Healthy soil means healthy plants, and that will attract even more butterflies and pollinators."

Lucy nodded, imagining how lush and welcoming her garden would be next spring. She felt a new appreciation for the quiet, steady work of autumn, knowing it was just as important as the vibrant growth of spring and summer.

Her dad joined them later, carrying a few bags of fallen leaves. "I saved these for you, Lucy," he said, grinning. "We can use them to make leaf mulch to protect the soil and plants from the cold."

Lucy was excited to use the colorful leaves, knowing they'd add a natural, cozy layer to her garden beds. Together, they spread the leaves around the base of the plants, creating a warm blanket for the garden. The reds, yellows, and browns added a final touch of autumn beauty to her garden, making it look as if it had been tucked in for a long nap.

Once everything was prepared, Lucy looked around, feeling a sense of calm and satisfaction. Her garden looked different now—quieter, simpler, but beautiful in a whole new way. She realized that every season had its purpose, and that autumn was a time for reflection, care, and gentle preparation.

That evening, as she sat by the garden with a mug of warm cider, Lucy thought about the journey her garden had taken through the year. She had watched flowers bloom, butterflies grow, and life transform. Now, she felt ready for the next phase, knowing that her garden was protected and cared for.

As she watched the sun set, casting a golden glow over the autumn leaves, Lucy whispered a soft thank-you to her garden, grateful for all it had given her. She knew that when spring arrived, her garden would awaken, stronger and more beautiful, ready to welcome her butterfly friends once again.

And until then, she would patiently wait, knowing that even in its quietest moments, her garden was alive, filled with the promise of life and renewal.

Chapter 23: Saving Seeds

As the days grew cooler, Lucy became more focused on preparing her garden for the winter. One morning, while inspecting the last few blooms, she noticed that many of her flowers had started to dry up and turn brown. Instead of feeling sad, Lucy felt a sense of excitement—this was her chance to save seeds for next year's garden. She'd recently learned from her mom that saving seeds was a wonderful way to keep her garden going and a sustainable way to preserve her favourite plants.

Eager to get started, Lucy grabbed a few small paper envelopes and a marker. She planned to collect seeds from the flowers she loved most: zinnias, marigolds, and cosmos. She thought about each flower and all the memories from the summer, and she felt a wave of gratitude. These seeds would be like little pieces of her garden's story, ready to be planted again in the spring.

Her mom joined her in the garden, showing her which parts of the flowers held the seeds. "Once flowers are done blooming, they often dry out and form seed heads," her mom explained, pointing to a dry zinnia bloom. "Inside are tiny seeds, each one with the potential to grow into a whole new plant next year."

Lucy carefully picked up a dried zinnia and looked at it closely, noticing the small, brown seeds tucked inside the bloom. She gently shook them out into her hand, marveling at how each seed was a miniature version of the future plant it would grow into. It felt like holding a little miracle in her palm.

"Isn't it amazing?" Lucy said, smiling. "These tiny seeds will grow into big, bright flowers next year!"

Her mom nodded, smiling proudly. "That's the magic of nature. By saving seeds, you're not only bringing your garden back, but you're also reducing the need to buy new plants. It's a sustainable way to garden, and it helps the environment."

Lucy loved the idea of sustainability—taking care of her garden in a way that was gentle on the earth and encouraged new life to grow. She carefully placed the zinnia seeds into a labelled envelope and moved on to the marigolds, feeling like she was gathering little treasures from her garden.

Next, she collected seeds from the marigolds, gently plucking out the slender, black and white seeds from the dried flower heads. She remembered how much her butterfly friends had loved these bright orange blooms, and she felt happy knowing that next year, she could bring back even more marigolds for them to enjoy.

As she moved on to the cosmos, she found their seeds—small and spiky—nestled inside the dried blooms. She carefully collected them, remembering the delicate pink and white flowers that had danced in the breeze all summer.

By the time she'd finished, Lucy had envelopes filled with seeds from each of her favourite flowers. She labelled each one with the flower's name and the year, imagining how satisfying it would be to open them in the spring and start her garden anew.

Her friends Mia, Ben, and Sophia stopped by later, curious about what she was up to. Lucy eagerly showed them the envelopes and explained how she'd collected seeds from her garden.

"This is so cool, Lucy!" Ben said, examining the seeds. "It's like you're saving pieces of your garden for next year."

Mia nodded, her eyes wide with interest. "I didn't know you could just collect seeds like this. So you're growing next year's garden from the same plants?"

Lucy grinned, feeling proud of her little collection. "Exactly! It's a way to keep the garden going and save resources. Plus, I get to grow the same flowers I loved this year."

Sophia looked thoughtful. "It's like recycling, but for flowers. That's really smart—and kind to the earth."

Lucy beamed, happy to share her new knowledge about sustainability with her friends. She explained how saving seeds helped reduce waste and how it ensured her garden would have the same flowers the butterflies loved. It was a way to give back to nature while creating something beautiful.

Later, as Lucy stored her seed envelopes in a cool, dry place, she thought about the cycle of life her garden had taught her. Each flower had bloomed, provided food and beauty, and then left behind seeds—tiny bundles of life ready to start again. It felt comforting to know that her garden's story would continue, carried forward in these seeds.

Her mom joined her, giving her a hug. "You've done something wonderful, Lucy. These seeds are more than just for next year's garden—they're a reminder of everything you've learned this season about nature, growth, and caring for the earth."

Lucy felt a warm glow of pride. She had started with a simple garden, but it had grown into something meaningful, filled with life, beauty, and purpose. As she looked at her envelopes, she felt a renewed sense of responsibility to nurture her garden with care and kindness, knowing that each small act made a difference.

And as the days grew colder, Lucy felt content, knowing that her garden's future was safe in those tiny seeds. They were a promise of new beginnings, of flowers blooming, butterflies returning, and a garden that would keep growing, year after year, rooted in love and sustainability.

Chapter 24: The Butterfly Garden Club

With autumn fully settled and her garden prepared for the winter, Lucy found herself missing the excitement of butterflies and blooming flowers. She loved how much she had learned from her garden and the joy of sharing it with friends, family, and neighbours. As she thought about her experiences, an idea began to form in her mind. What if she could keep the magic of her butterfly garden alive, even in the cooler months, by sharing it with even more people?

One afternoon, while working on a school assignment, Lucy's idea came to life: she could start a Butterfly Garden Club at school. It would be a place where she could share what she'd learned about butterflies, gardening, and sustainability with her classmates. Together, they could explore the wonders of nature and even help others start their own gardens!

The next day, she excitedly told her teacher, Ms. Martinez, about her idea.

"That's a wonderful idea, Lucy!" Ms. Martinez said, smiling warmly. "A club like this could bring together students who love nature and want to learn more about caring for the environment. Plus, it's a great way to spread awareness about butterflies and the important role they play in our ecosystem."

With Ms. Martinez's support, Lucy began making plans to start the Butterfly Garden Club. She created a flyer with bright colors and pictures of butterflies and flowers, hoping to catch the interest of her classmates. At the top, she wrote:

Join the Butterfly Garden Club!

Explore the world of butterflies, learn about gardening, and help nature thrive!

Lucy posted the flyers around the school and eagerly awaited the first meeting, excited to see who would come. When the day finally arrived, she walked into the classroom she'd reserved for the club, feeling a mix of excitement and nerves. To her delight, a group of classmates, including her friends Mia, Ben, and Sophia, were already there, chatting excitedly.

Once everyone was settled, Lucy stood at the front of the room and introduced the club. "Thank you all for coming! The Butterfly Garden Club is a place where we can learn about butterflies, gardening, and ways to help the environment. I started my own butterfly garden this year, and it's been amazing. I'd love to share what I've learned and help you all start your own gardens, too."

The group listened attentively as Lucy shared stories of her garden, her butterflies, and the journey she had taken to create a haven for pollinators. She explained the butterfly life cycle, from tiny eggs to caterpillars, chrysalises, and, finally, butterflies. She showed them sketches from her notebook and photos of her garden in full bloom, and even shared her story of watching her caterpillar friend Curly transform into a butterfly.

After her introduction, Lucy asked the group if anyone had questions or ideas they'd like to explore. To her surprise, hands shot up all around the room.

"Can we learn to grow plants from seeds?" a classmate named Ella asked. "I've always wanted to start a garden, but I don't know how."

Lucy grinned. "Definitely! We'll have a seed-planting day in the spring so we can all grow flowers that butterflies love."

Ben chimed in, "Can we talk about ways to help the environment, too? Like saving seeds or using compost?"

Lucy nodded enthusiastically. "Absolutely! We'll cover gardening tips, but we can also learn about things like composting and reducing waste. Gardening isn't just about growing flowers—it's about taking care of the earth, too."

The room buzzed with excitement as Lucy and her friends brainstormed ideas for the club. They decided to meet once a week, with each meeting focused on a different topic: butterfly facts, seed saving, flower types, and even a session on designing a garden layout. They also planned a field trip to a local botanical garden in the spring to see different flowers and plants up close.

As the weeks passed, the Butterfly Garden Club became the highlight of Lucy's school days. Each meeting was filled with laughter, curiosity, and a shared love for nature. Her classmates enjoyed learning new things, and many of them started collecting seeds from their own flowers at home, eager to plant them in the spring.

Lucy created a "Butterfly Club Bulletin Board" at school, where members could share their drawings, photos, and facts they'd learned. Each member contributed, and soon the board was covered with colorful pictures of butterflies, labelled flower drawings, and even poems about nature. It had become a place where the whole school could learn a little bit more about the beauty of butterflies and gardens.

As winter approached, Lucy planned a special club project: creating "butterfly-friendly" garden kits to share with other students in the spring. Each kit would include a packet of seeds, instructions on how to start a butterfly garden, and a few fun facts about butterflies. Lucy and her friends spent hours preparing these kits, knowing that they would help even more students create a safe haven for butterflies.

One afternoon, as she and her friends were assembling the kits, Mia turned to her and said, "Lucy, this club is amazing. You've brought the magic of your garden to all of us. I can't wait to plant these seeds and watch butterflies visit my garden."

Lucy felt a surge of happiness, realizing that her small garden project had grown into something much bigger—a community of young gardeners, all learning to appreciate and protect nature. She thought about the butterflies she had nurtured, knowing that by helping her classmates create butterfly gardens, she was ensuring that these special creatures would always have safe places to thrive.

On the last day of the club before winter break, Lucy gathered everyone together for a special thank-you. "I'm so grateful to each of you for joining the Butterfly Garden Club," she said, her voice full of warmth. "This year, we've learned a lot, shared stories, and grown closer to nature. Next spring, we'll start planting together, and I know our gardens will be amazing."

Her classmates clapped and cheered, and Lucy felt a deep sense of accomplishment. The club had not only given her a chance to share her love of butterflies and gardening, but it had also helped her form friendships with others who shared her passion for protecting nature.

As Lucy walked home that day, she felt excited for the future. The Butterfly Garden Club had brought a new purpose to her love for nature, showing her that even small acts—like planting a flower, saving a seed, or sharing a fact—could create ripples of change.

And as she looked ahead to spring, Lucy knew her journey with the Butterfly Garden Club had only just begun. Together, they would grow new gardens, welcome more butterflies, and continue their mission to protect and celebrate the beauty of nature, one flower and butterfly at a time.

Chapter 25: Building a Butterfly House

As the days grew shorter and the chilly autumn rains began to fall, Lucy thought more about the butterflies and how they might find shelter in the wetter, colder months. She remembered watching her butterfly friends, like Sunny and Flash, seek cover under leaves during rain showers in the summer. Now that it was cooler and wetter, she wanted to create a safe place for any butterflies still visiting her garden.

One evening, while reading a gardening book, Lucy found a section about building a butterfly house. Her eyes lit up as she imagined a cozy little shelter for butterflies, a place where they could rest safely during rainy days. She decided that this would be her next project—a small butterfly house, handcrafted with love for her garden visitors.

The next weekend, Lucy told her parents about her idea. "I'd like to build a butterfly house for the garden," she said. "It would be a place where butterflies can shelter from the rain and the cold."

Her dad smiled. "That sounds like a great idea, Lucy. Let's gather some materials and make a plan."

Lucy sketched out a design for the butterfly house. She imagined a small, wooden structure with thin vertical slits for butterflies to enter but narrow enough to keep out rain and wind. Inside, she planned to place thin branches and bits of bark, which would give butterflies something to grip onto and make it feel like a natural hiding place.

Once she had her design ready, Lucy and her dad went to the hardware store to pick up the materials. They gathered a few wooden boards, waterproof paint, and some nails. Lucy was excited as she imagined how cozy and inviting the house would be.

Back home, she and her dad got to work. First, they measured and cut the wood according to her design. Lucy watched carefully as her dad showed her how to hammer the nails gently, making sure each piece was secure. Together, they built a small rectangular box, leaving the front open with several thin vertical slits that would allow butterflies to enter.

Once the structure was built, Lucy sanded the edges carefully, making sure there were no rough spots. She chose a soft, natural color of waterproof paint that would blend into her garden, helping the house feel like part of the natural landscape. As she painted, she imagined the butterflies finding this cozy little shelter, a safe spot to rest during storms.

The next day, after the paint had dried, Lucy added some finishing touches. She gathered small pieces of bark, thin branches, and even a few pinecones from the yard, arranging them inside the house. The bark and branches would give the butterflies something to cling to, making the house feel more like a natural habitat.

When her friends Mia, Ben, and Sophia stopped by, they were immediately curious about her project.

"Is that for butterflies?" Sophia asked, peeking inside the little house.

Lucy nodded, beaming. "Yes! It's a butterfly house. I read that butterflies need shelter during cold and rainy weather, so I wanted to create a safe place for them to rest."

Ben looked impressed. "That's awesome, Lucy! It's like you're creating a little hotel for butterflies."

Mia grinned. "Do you think they'll really use it?"

Lucy smiled, feeling hopeful. "I think so. Butterflies naturally look for sheltered spots, and if they're still around during the cooler months, this house will give them a cozy place to stay."

Together, they carried the butterfly house into the garden and found the perfect spot near the butterfly bush. Lucy placed it on a sturdy post, just above the flowers, and made sure it was angled slightly forward to prevent rain from getting inside. She hoped the nearby blooms would make it easy for butterflies to spot the house whenever they needed shelter.

In the following days, Lucy watched eagerly to see if any butterflies would use the house. Every time it rained, she would check to see if she could spot any little wings resting inside. She imagined her butterfly friends, finding warmth and safety within the shelter she had built with care.

One rainy afternoon, as she checked the butterfly house, Lucy noticed a small flutter of orange inside. Her heart leapt with joy as she peered closer—it was a monarch butterfly, clinging to one of the branches, its wings folded close. She felt a wave of pride and happiness, knowing that her house had provided a safe place for a butterfly in need.

"Mom! Dad! There's a butterfly inside!" she called excitedly.

Her parents joined her, smiling as they saw the tiny monarch sheltered inside the house. "You've created something wonderful, Lucy," her mom said warmly. "This butterfly house is going to help keep your garden friends safe all year round."

As autumn continued, Lucy noticed that more butterflies stopped by the house, especially during rainy or windy days. It became a quiet, cozy corner of her garden, a place where her butterfly friends could find rest and shelter whenever they needed it.

The butterfly house quickly became one of Lucy's favourite parts of the garden. She loved knowing that even when the weather was rough, her butterflies had a place to stay safe. And as the cooler months settled in, she felt a deep sense of accomplishment, knowing that her garden had become a true haven for nature—a place of beauty, care, and warmth for every visitor.

As Lucy looked out at her garden, she felt grateful for all the lessons she'd learned about helping nature and giving back. She knew that every small act of kindness she showed to her garden, from planting flowers to building a butterfly house, was a way of creating a welcoming world for all creatures, great and small.

And with that, Lucy knew her garden's story would continue, season after season, growing richer and more meaningful with each thoughtful change she made.

Chapter 26: Lessons in Letting Go

As autumn deepened, Lucy noticed her garden entering a quiet, reflective phase. The flowers she had lovingly tended all summer were now shedding petals, their colors fading as they prepared to rest through the winter. The butterflies visited less frequently, and though she loved seeing her garden friends, she knew it was nearly time for most of them to move on.

One cool afternoon, Lucy sat in her garden, watching the last few butterflies fluttering between the remaining blooms. She felt a mixture of pride and sadness, knowing that soon, her garden would be still, waiting for spring's return. She had read about the butterfly life cycle so many times and had even watched her caterpillar friend Curly transform, but this year, the reality of letting go felt different. She now truly understood the beauty of each butterfly's journey and how her garden played a small, yet meaningful role in it.

As she watched the butterflies, Lucy's mom came outside and joined her. "Thinking about your butterflies, Lucy?" she asked gently.

Lucy nodded, feeling a bit emotional. "I know they have to leave to survive, and I'm glad they have warm places to go. But it's hard to let them go after spending the whole summer together. They're like my little garden family."

Her mom wrapped an arm around her. "I understand. You've cared for them and created a safe place for them to grow. But you know, letting go is a part of their life cycle. It's a way of giving them freedom to continue their journey."

Lucy thought about this, remembering everything she had learned about monarch migration. The butterflies she had nurtured were off to join thousands of others, flying south to warmer climates where they could thrive through the winter. It was an incredible journey, one that only a few creatures could make, and she felt a sense of awe at their strength and resilience.

Her mom continued, "Each butterfly carries a piece of your garden, Lucy. They're a part of this place, and by letting them go, you're helping them fulfil their purpose."

Lucy nodded, feeling a small sense of comfort. "I like to think they remember my garden as they fly. And when they return, it will feel like welcoming back old friends."

The thought of welcoming new butterflies, possibly even descendants of the ones she had seen this summer, filled her with hope. The cycle would continue, and her garden would once again be a place of beauty and transformation.

To help herself process the bittersweet emotions of saying goodbye, Lucy decided to document everything she had learned about the butterfly life cycle in her notebook. She drew each stage again—the tiny egg, the growing caterpillar, the delicate chrysalis, and finally, the butterfly. Next to each drawing, she added notes and little memories of her time with the butterflies. She described Sunny, Flash, Curly, and all the other butterflies she had named and loved, knowing that these memories would keep them close, even after they were gone.

Later that week, as Lucy watched the last monarchs of the season flutter away, she whispered a gentle farewell. "Safe travels, my friends. Thank you for visiting my garden, for showing me so much beauty. I'll see you again someday."

Her friends Mia, Ben, and Sophia stopped by to visit the garden one last time before winter. They joined her in saying goodbye to the butterflies, each of them touched by the experience. Mia held Lucy's hand, giving it a squeeze. "You've given them a wonderful home, Lucy. They'll be back, or maybe their children will. Either way, they'll remember this place."

Lucy smiled, feeling the weight of her friends' words. She realized that letting go didn't have to mean losing something—it could also mean giving something beautiful the freedom to grow and continue its journey.

As the leaves turned shades of amber and red, Lucy spent time adding the final touches to her garden. She planted a few bulbs for spring, tended to the soil, and checked on the butterfly house, making sure it was ready for any late travellers seeking shelter. Her garden, now quieter, held a different kind of beauty, a stillness that reminded her of how life could change and evolve while still remaining part of something larger.

On the last day of October, Lucy wrote a short entry in her notebook, reflecting on her summer of butterflies and blooms:

"Today, I learned that letting go is part of the journey. The butterflies have left my garden, but they carry its love with them, flying freely into the world. And when spring returns, I'll welcome new butterflies with open arms, knowing each one has a story to tell, a journey to make. My garden is a place where life begins, transforms, and takes flight, and I am grateful to be part of that magic."

As Lucy closed her notebook, she looked around at her garden, feeling a deep sense of peace. She understood now that letting go was not the end—it was the start of something new, a continuation of the cycle she had come to cherish.

She whispered one last farewell to her butterfly friends, her heart light and full. And as the autumn breeze swept through her garden, she felt ready for the quiet season ahead, trusting that life, in all its beauty and change, would return to her garden in time.

Chapter 27: A Winter Garden Plan

With the butterflies gone and the colder days settling in, Lucy found herself missing the colours and life that had filled her garden all summer. But rather than feeling sad, she felt inspired to create a winter garden that could withstand the cold while keeping her little haven alive. She realized that just because it was winter didn't mean her garden had to go dormant entirely. Some plants could thrive even in chilly weather, providing beauty and support for winter wildlife.

One snowy afternoon, Lucy sat at the kitchen table with her gardening notebook, jotting down ideas and sketching out a plan. Her mom joined her with a cup of tea and looked over her shoulder. "Planning your winter garden, I see?" she asked with a smile.

Lucy nodded, her eyes sparkling with excitement. "Yes! I want to add plants that can survive the cold and maybe even add a little color to the garden. Plus, some winter plants could be helpful for birds or insects that stick around."

Her mom smiled proudly, pulling out one of her gardening books. "That sounds wonderful, Lucy. You know, evergreen plants are a great way to keep your garden green all year. And certain winter berries can provide food for birds and add color even in the snow."

Lucy loved the idea of creating a winter garden that could support wildlife while keeping her garden beautiful. She opened her notebook and wrote down a few goals for her winter garden:

Choose Evergreen Plants: Add greenery that will stay lush throughout the winter.

Incorporate Winter Berries: Include plants with berries that provide food for birds.

Create Shelter for Wildlife: Keep some areas undisturbed for animals seeking winter shelter.

Add a Pop of Color: Find plants with bright hues that look beautiful against the snow.

With her goals in mind, Lucy and her mom researched a few plants that would work well in her garden. After browsing through the gardening book and looking online, they made a list of options:

Wintergreen: A low-growing plant with dark green leaves and bright red berries. It was perfect for adding a splash of color, and the berries would be a treat for birds.

Holly Bush: Known for its thick, green leaves and clusters of red berries, holly would provide both shelter and food for winter birds.

Hellebores (Winter Roses): These flowers could bloom even in winter, adding a delicate touch of pink and white to the garden when everything else was frosty.

Snowdrops: Small, white flowers that would peek out of the snow in early spring, signalling that winter was ending and spring was near.

Pine Sprigs and Conifers: Hardy evergreens that would keep the garden looking lush and green even in the coldest months.

With her list ready, Lucy and her mom headed to the local nursery to see if they could find any winter plants. The nursery had a section dedicated to hardy winter plants, and Lucy felt a thrill of excitement as she browsed the selection. She chose a small holly bush, a few wintergreen plants, and a bundle of hellebores, already picturing where each plant would go in her garden.

Back home, Lucy and her mom bundled up in coats and gloves to start planting. Together, they dug small holes in the garden beds, carefully placing each plant in its new spot. She chose a corner for the holly bush, imagining how beautiful the green and red would look against the snow. The wintergreen plants she arranged near her butterfly house, creating a cozy, welcoming spot for any small birds or creatures that needed shelter.

As she planted the hellebores, Lucy felt excited knowing that her winter garden would still have a few blossoms, even during the colder months. She pictured their soft, pink petals standing out against the snowy ground, bringing a little touch of color and warmth to her garden.

To complete her winter garden, Lucy added a layer of mulch around the new plants, insulating the roots to protect them from frost. She remembered from her autumn preparations that mulch would also enrich the soil, giving the plants a healthy start when spring returned.

Her dad joined them outside, carrying a small bird feeder he had picked up at the nursery. "I thought this might add a little extra life to your winter garden, Lucy," he said, handing it to her. "Birds will love visiting, and they'll appreciate the food when it gets really cold."

Lucy's face lit up as she took the feeder. "Thank you, Dad! I'll put it near the holly bush. I bet it will attract some of the local birds."

They filled the feeder with birdseed and hung it on a low branch of the holly bush, making sure it was easy for birds to spot. Lucy felt a sense of joy as she looked around her winter garden, imagining how it would look once the snow arrived. Even in the quiet of winter, her garden would be a place of life, color, and warmth for any creatures passing through.

That night, Lucy added a new entry to her gardening notebook: "Today, I planted my winter garden. It's small but strong, and I hope it brings comfort and color to the garden through the cold months. I'm excited to see the holly and wintergreen berries, to watch the birds find shelter, and to see the snowdrops peek out when spring arrives. My garden is changing with the seasons, and I love knowing it will always be alive in some way."

As the first snowflakes fell later that week, Lucy watched from her window, admiring her little winter garden. She spotted a few birds hopping around the holly bush, pecking at the berries and seeds she had left for them. The evergreen leaves stood out brightly against the fresh snow, making her garden look like a hidden winter oasis.

Lucy felt a sense of pride and joy, knowing that her garden could adapt to any season. It had blossomed with life in the summer, gently transformed in the autumn, and now stood strong and welcoming in the winter. And as she watched the snow blanket her winter garden, Lucy felt grateful for the lessons her garden continued to teach her—the beauty of change, the strength in resilience, and the joy of creating a home for life, no matter the season.

Chapter 28: A Visit to the Butterfly Conservatory

One chilly Saturday morning, Lucy's parents surprised her with an unexpected outing. "Lucy, get ready," her mom said, smiling. "We're taking you somewhere special today."

Lucy's eyes sparkled with excitement as she wondered where they could be going. They bundled up, climbed into the car, and drove through the snowy town until they reached a large glass building with a sign that read: "Butterfly Conservatory." Lucy's heart leapt with joy. She'd heard about conservatories before but had never been to one. Inside, butterflies from all over the world lived in a warm, lush environment, even in the cold of winter.

Her dad winked at her as they walked toward the entrance. "We thought you'd like to see some butterflies, even though it's winter outside."

Lucy could hardly contain her excitement as they entered the conservatory. She stepped into a warm, tropical room filled with vibrant flowers, towering plants, and butterflies flitting through the air in every direction. The air was filled with the delicate scent of blossoms, and the sunlight streaming through the glass ceiling made the whole place feel like a hidden paradise.

"Wow..." Lucy whispered, gazing around in awe. Butterflies of every color and pattern floated around her, landing gently on flowers and plants. It felt like stepping into a dream.

A friendly guide approached, noticing Lucy's wonder. "Welcome to the Butterfly Conservatory! Would you like a tour? I'd be happy to show you around and introduce you to some of our butterfly friends."

Lucy nodded eagerly, and her parents smiled as they followed the guide into a nearby exhibit. As they walked, the guide pointed out different species and shared interesting facts about each one.

"This here is a Blue Morpho," the guide said, pointing to a large butterfly with shimmering, electric blue wings. "These butterflies come from the rainforests of Central and South America. When they open their wings, they're bright blue, but when they close them, the color changes to brown, making it easier for them to blend in and hide from predators."

Lucy was fascinated as she watched the Blue Morpho flutter gracefully from one plant to another, its wings like flashes of sky against the green leaves. She thought about how amazing it was that each butterfly had unique adaptations, suited to their environment.

As they continued, they entered an area filled with delicate, translucent butterflies that seemed to glow in the light. The guide explained, "These are Glasswing butterflies from Central America. Their wings are nearly transparent, which helps them stay hidden from predators. It's one of nature's clever ways to help them survive."

Lucy's eyes widened as she marvelled at the glass-like wings. She loved learning about how each butterfly had its own way of surviving in the world, from vibrant colors to mimicry and camouflage.

The guide then led them to a corner of the conservatory with tall, leafy plants covered in clusters of small, brightly coloured butterflies. "These are Painted Ladies. They're found in many parts of the world, and they're known for their long migrations, just like monarch butterflies."

Hearing this reminded Lucy of her own butterfly friends back in her garden and their journey south for the winter. She felt a pang of longing to see her butterflies again, but learning about other species who also migrated made her feel connected to them, as if each butterfly was part of a larger, global family.

As they walked, Lucy spotted a cluster of smaller, jewel-toned butterflies called Emerald Swallowtails. The guide explained that these butterflies were native to Asia and had bright, iridescent green wings that shimmered in the light.

"They're like little flying emeralds!" Lucy exclaimed, enchanted by the way the butterflies sparkled.

Toward the end of the tour, the guide brought them to a "butterfly nursery" where chrysalises hung delicately from branches, each one shimmering with hues of green, gold, and brown. "This is where we raise butterflies from eggs to adulthood," the guide explained. "These chrysalises will eventually hatch, releasing new butterflies into the conservatory."

Lucy gazed at the chrysalises, memories of Curly's transformation in her garden flooding back. She felt a sense of wonder knowing that each of these chrysalises held a butterfly waiting to emerge. It reminded her of the resilience and beauty of the life cycle she had come to love.

At the end of the tour, the guide invited Lucy to visit the "Butterfly Garden," an area filled with flowers that butterflies loved, such as milkweed, coneflowers, and lantanas. Lucy smiled, recognizing many of the plants from her own garden. She felt a deep sense of pride, knowing that her little backyard garden was connected to this larger world of butterfly conservation.

As they left the garden, Lucy turned to the guide with a bright smile. "Thank you for sharing all of this with us. I love butterflies, and I'm starting a club at my school to help people learn about them too!"

The guide smiled, clearly impressed. "That's wonderful, Lucy! Butterflies need people who care about them, and you're making a big difference by teaching others. Every little garden and every act of kindness toward nature helps protect these beautiful creatures."

On the way home, Lucy couldn't stop talking about all the different butterflies she'd seen, each one as unique and special as the last. She felt inspired, not only to continue caring for her own garden but to share her new knowledge with her Butterfly Garden Club and encourage them to make small changes that could help butterflies everywhere.

As she lay in bed that night, Lucy imagined her garden in the spring, filled with vibrant blooms, fluttering wings, and maybe even new butterflies from faraway places. She dreamed of the day she might see Blue Morphos, Glasswings, and Emerald Swallowtails in her garden, knowing that her small piece of the world was part of a much bigger journey.

The visit to the conservatory had given her a deeper appreciation for butterflies of all shapes, sizes, and colors, and for the incredible diversity that nature had created. And with that, Lucy knew she would continue her journey, working to make her garden a place of refuge, beauty, and love—for every butterfly, near and far.

Chapter 29: An Unexpected Gift

As winter settled in and Lucy's garden lay quietly under a blanket of snow, she often found herself thinking back to the colorful days of summer. Memories of her butterflies—Sunny, Flash, and Curly—brought a smile to her face. She missed seeing them fluttering around, but the thought of their return in the spring filled her with excitement and anticipation.

One cozy evening, as she was finishing a sketch of a butterfly she'd seen at the conservatory, her mom walked in with a small box wrapped in soft, silver paper and tied with a delicate ribbon.

"Lucy, I have something special for you," her mom said, her eyes twinkling with warmth. "This is a little gift to remind you of the garden adventures you've had this year."

Lucy's curiosity sparked as she took the box from her mom. She untied the ribbon and carefully lifted the lid, her eyes widening in surprise. Inside was a beautiful silver necklace, and at the center hung a delicate butterfly charm. The wings of the butterfly were decorated with tiny, colorful stones—orange, blue, and green—that glistened softly in the light.

Lucy's heart filled with happiness as she gently lifted the necklace. "Oh, Mom, it's beautiful!" she whispered, her voice full of emotion. "Thank you so much!"

Her mom knelt beside her, placing a gentle hand on her shoulder. "This butterfly charm is a little reminder of all the special moments you've had in the garden this year. You've learned so much, not only about butterflies and plants but about resilience, patience, and kindness. I thought this might be a way for you to keep those memories close, even during the winter."

Lucy felt a warmth in her heart as she thought about the journey her garden had taken her on. The charm seemed to hold every memory—from planting the first flowers to seeing Curly transform into a butterfly, to the visit to the conservatory and learning about butterflies from all over the world. She felt as if the necklace held all the love and beauty of her garden within its tiny, shimmering wings.

Her mom helped her put on the necklace, and Lucy touched the charm, feeling its cool, smooth surface resting just above her heart. It felt comforting, as if her butterflies were right there with her, reminding her of everything she had experienced and learned.

"I'll wear this every day, Mom," Lucy said, smiling up at her. "It'll remind me to keep learning and to care for nature. And whenever I see a butterfly, I'll think of my garden and all the wonderful memories we've made."

Her mom hugged her tightly. "I'm so proud of you, Lucy. You've created something beautiful with your garden, and that beauty lives on in every act of kindness you show to the world around you."

Over the next few days, Lucy wore her necklace everywhere. It quickly became a symbol of her love for nature and her commitment to helping butterflies and other creatures. She showed it to her friends at the Butterfly Garden Club, explaining how each color in the charm reminded her of a special part of her garden—the orange of Sunny's wings, the blue of the sky, and the green of the leaves.

The charm also inspired her to think about new ways to expand her garden in the spring. She wrote in her notebook about planting even more flowers, maybe even adding a small water feature for birds and butterflies to drink from. Each time she touched the charm, she felt inspired to keep growing, learning, and finding ways to bring more life to her garden.

One snowy afternoon, as she sat by the window watching the winter birds peck at her bird feeder, Lucy held the butterfly charm in her hand and smiled. She knew her garden's story was far from over. This necklace was not just a reminder of the past but a symbol of everything yet to come—the flowers, the butterflies, the seasons of growth and change.

And as she dreamed of the spring days ahead, Lucy felt a deep sense of gratitude for the journey her garden had taken her on, knowing that it had become more than just a place for plants and butterflies. It had become a part of her heart, a place of joy, wonder, and endless possibility.

Chapter 30: Spring Preparations

The first hints of spring began to creep into the air, melting the last traces of winter snow and filling Lucy's garden with a soft, earthy scent. The sun stayed out a bit longer each day, and tiny buds started to peek out from the branches. Lucy's heart swelled with excitement—soon, her garden would come back to life.

One sunny morning, she put on her butterfly charm necklace and headed outside, feeling the familiar sense of joy that came with working in her garden. She carefully removed the layer of mulch she had added in the fall, uncovering the soil beneath and spotting the first signs of green sprouting from her winter plants. Her wintergreen and holly bush looked vibrant, and the hellebores were already starting to bloom, their soft pink and white petals adding a gentle touch of color.

Lucy grabbed her gardening notebook and began planning her new additions for the year. She had saved seeds from her favourite summer flowers—zinnias, marigolds, and cosmos—and was excited to see them bloom again. She carefully sketched a new layout, adding a few new plants that she hoped would attract even more butterflies and pollinators. This year, she decided, her garden would be bigger and brighter than ever.

As she worked, Lucy's friends Mia, Ben, and Sophia stopped by, each eager to see her plans for the garden's revival.

"Are you going to bring back Sunny's flowers?" Mia asked, smiling as she looked over Lucy's notebook.

Lucy nodded, grinning. "Definitely! I saved seeds from all of our favourite flowers. I even thought about adding a few new ones, like milkweed and asters, to attract even more butterflies."

Ben's eyes lit up. "Milkweed? That's great! Monarch butterflies love milkweed. You might get even more visitors this year."

Sophia pointed to a spot on the garden layout where Lucy had drawn a small, shallow dish. "Is this for water?" she asked.

Lucy nodded. "Yes! I read that butterflies need places to drink water, especially when it's hot. I thought I'd make a little puddling station with rocks around it. That way, butterflies can rest and drink whenever they need to."

Her friends admired her plans, excited to see Lucy's garden come alive again. Together, they helped her dig small holes in the garden beds, preparing each spot for the seeds she would plant in a few weeks. As they worked, they reminisced about last summer, sharing stories of watching butterflies flutter from flower to flower and laughing about their favourite moments with Curly the caterpillar.

Lucy took a deep breath, feeling a sense of gratitude for her garden and the joy it had brought her and her friends. Her butterfly charm sparkled in the sunlight, a reminder of everything she had learned and the beauty of each season's cycle. She knew this year's garden would be even more special because she was bringing with her the memories, lessons, and love that her garden had taught her.

When her friends left, Lucy spent the afternoon carefully sprinkling seeds into the prepared soil. She patted the earth down gently, knowing that each tiny seed held the potential for new life. She imagined her garden in full bloom, filled with vibrant colors and fluttering wings, and felt a deep sense of peace.

That night, as she wrote in her notebook, Lucy reflected on her journey with the garden. She had started with a few flowers and a dream, but her garden had grown into something much more—a place of learning, connection, and beauty. She added one final note before turning off her light:

"Today, I prepared my garden for spring. Each seed I plant carries a memory of last year's flowers and butterflies. My garden is a part of me now, a place of growth, wonder, and friendship. I'm excited to see what this new season will bring."

As the days grew warmer, Lucy continued to tend to her garden, watering the soil and watching the first sprouts push through the earth.

She felt a thrill of excitement, knowing that soon, the butterflies would return. And with each bloom, she would welcome back the magic, beauty, and memories of her butterfly haven, ready to start a new chapter in her garden adventure.

Chapter 31: A Garden Full of Life

As spring unfolded, Lucy's garden burst into life, more vibrant and beautiful than she had ever imagined. The seeds she had carefully planted began to sprout, each one stretching toward the sun, filling her garden beds with rich shades of green. Within weeks, the flowers started to bloom—zinnias, marigolds, cosmos, milkweed, and asters painted the garden with bright, joyful colors.

One morning, as Lucy stepped outside, she was greeted by the soft hum of bees drifting from flower to flower, collecting pollen. A few ladybugs crawled along the leaves, adding tiny dots of red and black to the lush greenery. And then, in a moment of pure happiness, Lucy spotted the first butterfly of the season—a monarch with bright orange wings that floated gracefully around her garden.

"Welcome back," she whispered, watching the butterfly as it glided toward a patch of milkweed, delicately sipping nectar. Lucy's heart swelled with joy as she saw it land on the very plant she had planted specifically for monarchs. Her garden was alive again, and she felt the beauty of the cycle renewing itself before her eyes.

Her friends Mia, Ben, and Sophia soon arrived, as excited as Lucy to see the garden come to life.

"Look at all the colors!" Mia exclaimed, her eyes wide with wonder. "It's even more beautiful than last year."

Ben pointed to a group of butterflies fluttering around the asters. "Lucy, you've created a butterfly paradise! They love it here."

Sophia knelt down to inspect a cluster of blue and purple blooms. "The bees are everywhere too. You're helping so many creatures, Lucy. This garden is a little sanctuary."

Lucy smiled, feeling a deep sense of pride and happiness. Her garden was indeed a sanctuary, a place where creatures big and small could find food, shelter, and safety. And it wasn't just butterflies—her garden had drawn in all kinds of wildlife, each one adding its own rhythm to the lively atmosphere.

As the days passed, the garden grew even more lush and vibrant. Sunny, Flash, and many new butterflies drifted in and out, dancing through the flowers. Birds chirped from the branches of her holly bush, occasionally stopping to drink from the puddling station Lucy had set up. She even spotted a small frog nestled near the damp edges, a reminder of the hidden life that her garden sustained.

Every morning, Lucy would sit in her favourite observation spot, the butterfly charm around her neck glinting in the sunlight, and marvel at the diversity around her. She realized that her garden had grown into something more than she had ever expected. It had become an ecosystem, a small world of interconnected life, with each flower, insect, and animal playing its part.

One afternoon, her grandpa came by to visit. He looked around the garden, taking in the sight of the butterflies, bees, and blooms, and nodded approvingly.

"You've done an incredible job, Lucy," he said, smiling warmly. "This garden is full of life and joy. It's not only beautiful, but it's also a gift to nature."

Lucy beamed, feeling proud of all the hard work and care she had put into her garden. "Thank you, Grandpa. I've learned so much from taking care of it, and it makes me so happy to see all the creatures here."

Grandpa patted her shoulder. "That's the magic of a garden—it teaches you about patience, kindness, and how every small act can make a difference. You're not just growing flowers; you're creating a place for life to flourish."

As spring turned into early summer, Lucy's garden became the talk of the neighbourhood. Families would pause by her fence, admiring the blooms and the colorful flurry of butterflies. Sometimes children would ask to come inside, and Lucy would happily lead small "tours," showing them the different flowers and explaining how each one attracted certain pollinators. She felt a renewed sense of purpose, sharing her love of nature with others and inspiring them to create their own small sanctuaries.

One evening, as the sun set over her blooming garden, Lucy sat quietly, reflecting on the journey that had led her here. Her garden had transformed from a simple idea into a vibrant oasis, and it was filled with so much life, joy, and beauty. Every flower, butterfly, and buzzing bee was a reminder of the connection she had fostered with nature—a connection that continued to grow with each season.

Her butterfly charm sparkled softly against her chest, and she touched it, smiling as she thought of all the memories her garden had given her. It was a place of learning, laughter, growth, and change, a place where every creature found a welcome home.

And as she looked out at her garden, lush and full of life, Lucy felt grateful for the journey, knowing that her little haven would keep blossoming and thriving, season after season, carrying with it the magic of nature's endless cycle.

Chapter 32: The Legacy of Lucy's Butterfly Garden

As the warm days of summer continued, Lucy noticed something incredible happening in her community. Her garden, with its vibrant blooms, fluttering butterflies, and lively visitors, had become more than just her personal haven. Neighbours often stopped to admire it, and children from her school came to see the butterflies, bees, and flowers Lucy had lovingly cultivated. People began talking about her garden as something special—a symbol of beauty, kindness, and a love for nature.

One day, her teacher, Ms. Martinez, invited Lucy to share her gardening experience with the class. "Lucy, would you like to tell everyone about your butterfly garden?" Ms. Martinez asked, smiling. "I think it could inspire others to start gardens of their own."

Lucy felt a thrill of excitement. She prepared a small presentation, filling it with photos, drawings, and stories about her garden's journey. When she shared it with her classmates, they listened eagerly, their faces lighting up with curiosity.

"Wow, you have so many butterflies!" one of her classmates, Jamie, said. "How did you make them come to your garden?"

Lucy explained, "Butterflies love certain flowers, like zinnias, marigolds, and milkweed. When you plant these, you're inviting butterflies to visit because they love the nectar and need the plants to lay their eggs. Anyone can do it!"

After her presentation, several classmates came up to Lucy with more questions. Some even asked if they could visit her garden to learn more about which flowers to plant. Lucy was overjoyed. She realized that her garden was having an impact beyond her own backyard—it was inspiring others to bring a little piece of nature's beauty into their lives, too.

LUCY'S BUTTERFLY GARDEN

A few weeks later, Lucy's garden became part of a local community event. Her mom had spoken with some neighbours and suggested hosting a small "Garden Open Day" where families could walk through Lucy's garden and learn about butterfly-friendly plants, pollinators, and how to create simple gardens at home.

Lucy helped prepare for the event, creating colorful signs for each section of her garden, showing which flowers attracted butterflies, bees, and other helpful insects. She set up a small table with packets of seeds she had saved from her own plants—zinnias, cosmos, marigolds, and milkweed—each packet tied with a tiny ribbon. She also displayed her notebook, filled with sketches, notes, and stories about the life cycle of butterflies, her favourite garden visitors, and the journey her garden had taken.

When the Garden Open Day arrived, people of all ages came to visit. Families wandered through the rows of flowers, admiring the vibrant blooms and pausing to watch the butterflies flutter by. Lucy greeted everyone with a warm smile, guiding them through her garden and explaining which plants they could grow at home to attract pollinators.

One family was especially inspired. "Lucy, your garden is amazing," said a woman named Mrs. Ramirez, who had brought her two young children along. "I've always wanted to start a garden, but I didn't know where to begin. Now I feel like I can try it!"

Lucy handed her a packet of marigold seeds. "Start with these! They're easy to grow, and butterflies love them. Just plant them in a sunny spot, water them, and watch them bloom. And soon, you might see butterflies visiting, too!"

Lucy's friends also came by, proudly sharing their own garden projects they had started at home. Inspired by Lucy's Butterfly Garden Club, many of them had planted their own butterfly-friendly flowers. Some had small potted gardens on balconies, while others had set aside a patch of yard for pollinator plants. Lucy felt a deep sense of happiness, knowing her garden had sparked this wonderful ripple effect.

As the day drew to a close, Ms. Martinez approached Lucy with an idea. "Lucy, I think it would be wonderful to create a community butterfly garden. We could plant it near the school so students and neighbours could enjoy it year-round. Would you be interested in helping us plan it?"

Lucy's eyes widened with excitement. "Yes! I'd love that! We could plant all kinds of flowers for butterflies, bees, and even birds!"

With the community's support, Lucy and Ms. Martinez began organizing the community butterfly garden project. Together with volunteers from her school and neighbourhood, they chose a spot near the schoolyard. Lucy led the group in designing the layout, suggesting flowers, bushes, and trees that would not only attract pollinators but also add color and life to the area.

Over the next few weeks, Lucy worked with her classmates, teachers, and neighbours to plant the new garden. They created winding paths, colorful flower beds, and even added a few small signs with butterfly facts and fun gardening tips for anyone who visited. The butterfly charm around her neck sparkled in the sun as she worked, a constant reminder of how her own garden journey had led to this amazing community effort.

When the community butterfly garden was finally completed, it became a beloved spot in town. Families visited on weekends, children played nearby, and students often paused to watch the butterflies, bees, and birds that flocked to the flowers. The garden quickly became a symbol of unity and a reminder of how small actions—like planting a flower or creating a space for nature—could make a big difference.

Lucy's heart filled with joy each time she visited the garden, knowing she had helped create a lasting space for people and wildlife alike. Her butterfly garden had grown from a single patch of flowers into a legacy that touched the lives of others, inspiring them to connect with nature and appreciate its beauty.

One afternoon, as Lucy sat on a bench near the community garden, she took a deep breath, feeling grateful for her journey and the garden's impact on her community. She looked down at her butterfly charm, touching it gently, and smiled, knowing her garden's story would continue through every flower, every butterfly, and every person it inspired.

And as she watched a monarch butterfly drift gracefully across the garden, Lucy realized that her butterfly haven wasn't just a place—it was a legacy of love, learning, and endless possibilities, growing with each new season and blooming in the hearts of everyone who visited.

Disclaimer:

This book, Lucy's Butterfly Garden, is a work of fiction created to inspire curiosity, foster a love for nature, and encourage young readers to explore the wonders of the outdoors. While Lucy's gardening journey is based on general principles of gardening and butterfly care, specific methods and recommendations in this story are simplified for storytelling purposes.

Readers interested in creating their own butterfly gardens are encouraged to consult reputable sources or gardening experts for detailed guidance on local plants, insect care, and environmental impacts. Always use safe, eco-friendly practices to protect both the garden and its visitors.

The author and publisher assume no responsibility for any injuries or damages arising from any activities related to gardening or insect care inspired by this story. Butterfly havens and respect nature.